THESE STRANGE & MAGIC THINGS

ALSO BY PETER M. BALL

SHORT STORY COLLECTIONS

The Birdcage Heart & Other Strange Tales

Not Quite The End Of the World Just Yet: Short Stories & Strange Futures

KEITH MURPHY URBAN FANTASY THRILLERS

Exile

Frost

Crusade

MIRIAM ASTER NOVELLAS

Horn

Bleed

ESSAYS

You Don't Want To Be Published & Other Things Nobody Tells You When You First Start Writing

THESE STRANGE & MAGIC THINGS

SHORT STORIES

PETER M. BALL

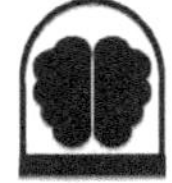

Brain Jar Press
PO Box 6687
Upper Mt Gravatt, QLD, 4122
Australia
www.BrainJarPress.com

Theses Strange And Magic Things, Copyright © 2020 by Peter M. Ball

Cover design by Brain Jar Press
Cover Image: *mystery woman holding the umbrella with black tentacles inside in the rainy night,* Tithi Luadthong/Shutterstock

ISBN: 978-1-922479-41-9

CONTENTS

Love is the Roar of a Chainsaw, Cutting Flesh in the Night — 1

One Last First Date Before The End Of The World — 5

The Place Beyond The Brambles — 15

Counting Down — 21

The Things You Do When the War Breaks Out — 27

Winged, With Sharp Teeth — 33

Upon Discovering a Ghost in the Five Star — 48

Tithes — 54

The Minotaurs & The Signal Ghosts — 74

Hornets Attack Your Best Friend Victor and Other Things We Called the Band — 78

Eight Minutes of Usable Daylight — 94

The Mike & Carly Story, Without The Gossip — 106

A White Cross Beside a Lonely Road — 116

Rule 34 — 138

Local Heroes — 142

Story Notes — 175

For my father, Terrance John Ball.
I couldn't have done it without you,

LOVE IS THE ROAR OF A CHAINSAW, CUTTING FLESH IN THE NIGHT

The whole thing kicked off as a joke—you know how these things go.

One of you says, "Let's start a zombie survival kit," and the other goes, "brilliant, we totally need to do that," and before you notice it six months have flashed by and you're treating the idea with deadly seriousness. Zombie apocalypse prep becomes the beating heart of your relationship. It binds you together in ways far stronger than saying "I love you" ever will. That's how everything started between me and Nat, a goofy comment made the first night we moved in together.

And it's not all bad, having a weird thing as a couple. The kit got us through the messy first weeks as we figured out how to cohabitate. That rough patch when you discover that one partner snores louder than any lumberjack, and the other partner's okay with accumulating pile of festering dishes by the sink, even though the dishwasher is right there underneath, empty and ready to load.

Cohabitation gets tricky, is what I'm saying. Finding an equilibrium took work in those early days,but every time we doubted our capacity to go the long haul, we'd remember the kit and the joy of planning and accumulating new gear to add. We'd remember why we loved each other and the doubts faded away.

. . .

We kicked our prep off by obtaining the usual basics, right off the CDC website: a few liters of purified water for each of us; sixteen tins of baked beans in ham sauce. Sanitation supplies: bleach and soap; a utility knife and duct tape; spare batteries for the maglite. We stored everything in two plastic crates, stacked beside the garage door. Easily found, in case of emergency. Habit and routine.

The kit became a private joke, but we always figured… one day, maybe? Not that we expected the walking dead, you understand, but a fire or an earthquake were feasible catastrphies and the principles were the same. One day, we'd be glad we built up our supplies. One day, it would come in handy.

Nat deployed the zombie survival kit as a talking point when meeting new people. She kept showing it off to visitors, seeing how they'd react. If they started lecturing us, banging on about zombies not being real, Nat took them off the list of friends we hung out with regularly. They were not our kind of people.

The kit also made shopping for presents easy. When Christmas arrived, Nat gave me a vintage Swiss army knife and a twenty-pack of glow sticks. I found her a personal water filter and two packs of weatherproof matches. We did everything as a joke at first, but jokes become tradition faster than you'd imagine. Every holiday became another opportunity. Every birthday, another thing added: signal flares; a repelling kit; four weeks' training at a wilderness survival camp, preparing for the collapse of civilization and the days when ransacking supermarket aisles ceased being a practical method of acquiring sustenance.

Then, on the day I turned thirty-six, Nat brought out the chainsaw. Twenty-five CCs of cutting power, a full complement of chipper teeth to help maintain the edge. A magnificent bit of gear, carefully selected and lovingly given.

Naturally, I made a stupid joke. The kit was our thing, and the goofiness of it bound Nat and I together. We didn't take it seriously, that wasn't the point. And for all a chainsaw had the weight of tradition, I'd grown used to extrapolating outwards, working through the just-in-cases of each new addition.

So I voiced the first question that popped into my head: "What happens when the fuel runs out? You might have gone for something manual, yeah?"

We'd fought before, me and Nat, but chainsaw debate got ugly. Three days of point, and counter-point, before we hit an impasse. Then I apologized for being a jerk, and Nat agreed to quit sleeping on the couch and come back to our bed.

Life returned to normal for a while.

And I figured we'd declared a truce, swear to fucking god. So I bought an axe for Nat's birthday and wrote "no fuel needed" on the card. A joke! Just being cute! Laughing about our silly thing!

Nat didn't see the humour.

It's been three weeks since Nat walked out. And, wow, you've got to admire the timing. The woman you love leaves and the dead rise from their graves. Nothing beats the apocalypse for kicking a man while he's down, you know?

I broke out the kit the moment I saw the news footage and thought, *Fuck me, that's a zombie.* Loaded things into the car and prepared to flee the city. We'd talked about it dozen times when putting together contingency plans. The first step is getting out of urban centers, putting distance between you and the dense population. Cities are full of walking snacks, who rapidly becoming walking threats after they get bit. It's zombie 101, man. Everybody knows it. Haul your ass and find an isolated place to hold up, preferably fortified.

But there's a difference between the smart thing and making the right choice. Pragmatism's an ugly way to live, and I figured Nat knows the kit is here. This glorious stash of gear we built together for just this circumstance. Nat's got to realize I won't leave without her, even if she's pissed at me.

So I wait, all kitted up for the end of the world, doing my best to discourage the zombies. Me, the axe, and the goddamn chainsaw Nat gifted me on my thirty-sixth birthday. The cutting teeth go through dead flesh and bone so easy, like chewing through soft liquorish.

The chainsaw hasn't run out of fuel yet. Three weeks, still going strong.

I doubt I'll get to apologize, but I won't stop waiting for the chance. Sitting here, praying that I'll see Nat soon. That we'll finally use our zombie emergency kit to live happily ever after.

For now, I'll express my love with the chainsaw's whine until Nat finds her way home.

ONE LAST FIRST DATE BEFORE THE END OF THE WORLD

When their night started, Logan worked to a simple plan: dinner; coffee; a short drive home. His date acknowledging this whole thing was a mistake, better-if-we-stay-friends, etcetera. Logan retreating to the share house on Talbot Street, settling in for a beer and debrief. His flatmate, Donna, telling Logan, *"I told you so."* Logan's date would forget him and go on with her life, and they would never speak again.

Instead, Logan's escorting Stina Herne along Currumbin Beach. Hitting the estuary and clambering onto the rocks. He figures the night is going well. The beach is a two-hour drive from the Thai restaurant, a fond memory from Logan's childhood mentioned over tom kha gai. A place Stina Herne suggested they visit right after he paid for the meal.

"It's a long drive," Logan said. "We'd arrive back late."

"I've got time," Stina Herne said, and that seemed like a good sign.

Currumbin Beach doesn't match Logan's memories. It used to be an open space, an unobstructed walk from car park to sand to water, all lit up by the moon overhead. Now spinifex and banksia smother the dunes, the new fences obscuring paths and view alike. The beach is brisk and damp and full of murder-alley gloom. Tainted with a faint scent that's more than salt spray and seaweed. Old bait, maybe? Or fish guts, discarded and left to rot after a fisherman sliced and scaled their catch?

Logan keeps returning to the same four words: cold, wet, dark, and frightening. Figures that combination is a fatality on the date front. The dark, alone, could be romantic. The cold and wet, less so. The threat of being murdered kills everything stone done, and the smell kills off any stray, amorous thoughts that survive everything else.

"Sorry," Logan says.

"For what?"

"For this. Currumbin wasn't like this, back when I lived here."

"It's fine."

"Perhaps." Logan rubs both hands together, glares at the murky waves rolling in. "The whole place is more feral than I remembered."

"Okay."

"I'm… embarrassed. I dragged you down here, promising something…"

Stina considers the ocean and the gloomy sky. "Relax," she says. "This is cool."

Logan doesn't relax, but he shuts up, at least. Knows it for the right play, despite his gut insisting otherwise. The stories he told over dinner focused on the beach in his memory: lights shining all the way to Surfers Paradise; the pleasure of climbing the Rock as a kid while his father went out to surf; nights spent there with dates throughout his teens, making out in the salt spray.

Now Logan's facing things forgotten about: the dangerous gleam of rocks in the moonlight, the wind cruel as a predator's tooth. The uneven surface isn't much fun to walk on and they're already damp.

He's weighed down by the sand in his sneakers. Logan can taste the sea on every breath.

Currumbin Rock is a chunk of black argillite. A relic left behind as the waves devoured the shoreline, pushing the cliffs further and further way from the sand. Transformed the towering heights into a stunted hill tucked beyond the parks and resorts and surf clubs, a place to get a decent view if you've got the money.

The Rock and the estuary didn't soften with age. They're all sharp edges and sharper angles. The Rock like a spear-tip aimed inland. Its slope is steep, but Logan climbed it as a kid. Went up, quick and easy, and perched on the apex. King of the World, no worries to plague him.

Except that Logan was younger. Lighter and fearless with youth. Now Logan pulls his jacket close, skin tightening as the frigid wind rips past. He looks up the slope, sixteen feet high, and pictures them slipping off.

"We'd break our necks getting up there," he says.

His date shrugs. "I'm game."

"You sure?"

Stina Herne puts both hands on the Rock, searching for handholds. "You raved about the view, yeah?"

"I did," Logan says. "The beach is just... not how I remembered it."

Stina Herne looks back and flashes a grin that softens the anxiety roiling through Logan's stomach. He fell hard for that smile before anything, when they first met at the café. His brain linking up the details in the seconds that followed: incredible grin plus silver hair plus raven tattooed on her left shoulder. Tall and pale and dangerously pretty. Logan going from *stranger* to *smitten* in record time. His flatmate Donna standing right beside him, putting two and two together. Delivering her immediate warning: "Don't date the goth chicks, buddy. No way you'll keep up with her."

Logan ignored that advice. Nutted up and asked Stina out cold, before his nerve failed and common sense overruled his desire.

Now, on the beach, Logan figures Donna's right. His fingers are numb, just from walking out across the sand, and he doesn't want to climb a great chunk of damp argillite in the dark. But Stina Lorne's already going up, searching for fresh handholds, the toes of her boots digging into the pitted surface.

"Come on," Stina says, and Logan follows. The stone is coarse beneath his fingers, like a calcified sponge. The wind slices past them and the sea roars, but the moon is full and bright, and he can identify a route up well enough. His pulse hammers, but they make it up and they huddle just shy of the tip. Young lovers perched side-by-side, exposed to the cruel gusts and bluster coming in across the water. The Surfers Paradise lights *are* pretty, but the darkness out over the surf is just as beautiful.

"This isn't so bad," Stina Herne says, but her shoulders tremble and she's breathing warmth into numb fingers.

"A-huh." Logan's contemplating the fall again. Or, truth be told, he's mulling over the landing, and the breaking, and the bleeding, and the pain. Oh god, so much pain before death.

"Why did this place matter to you?" Stina rubs her hands and breathes on them again. "Why here? What's the attraction?"

Logan sucks in a deep breath. Exhales, quietly. "We came out here as kids. Me and my parents. They told me the lights were fairy land."

Stina Herne peers into the distance, frowning. "Fairies are fond of neon?"

"I was seven. They were my mum and dad."

"Ah," Stina says, and grins. "So you were a trusting kid."

"I guess."

"A trusting adult, too," she says.

"How so?"

"Well... I mean, here we are," Stina says, "two hour's drive from dinner. You're climbing rocks in the dark beside a woman you don't know. I could be crazy, up here. I could push you off and roll your corpse into the sea and walk off while you bled and water filled your lungs. Nobody would ever figure what truly happened, would they?"

She says it with poise and calm, as if such things were probable. Logan grips the Rock a little tighter, digs his sneakers against the pitted stone. "I guess not," he says.

Stina Herne nods once, for emphasis. "See, trusting."

"Okay." Logan sucks in a short, nervous breath and says, "So... are you planning on doing that?"

Stina tilts her head back and smiles up at the moon. "No more than you are," she says.

"Cool."

They settle in there, on the Rock. Listen to each other breathe. It's so cold, their exhalations plume. Logan's hands are raw from the climb. They ache beneath the numbness.

"Besides," Stina says, breaking the stillness, "the same is true for me. This could be the moment you reveal you're all kinds of homicidal. I'm taking a risk with you, as much as you're taking one being up here with me."

More, Logan's subconscious whispers, but he doesn't say it out loud. It's a thought inspired by bad assumptions, old gender roles and toxic thinking. You're not automatically secure just because you're a dude. Play it careful. Play it safe.

Logan wishes he could kiss her, despite the conversation, but the moment doesn't seem right yet. Instead, he says, "I've got no plans to kill you, either."

Stina Herne adopts a smile that would do the Mona Lisa proud. "Wouldn't matter if you did."

It's not the response Logan expected. "No?"

"Not at all," Stina Herne says, the words so terribly certain. Logan's guts clench in panic as he wonders if Donna was right.

"You want to die or something?"

"No," Stina says, "it's just—" She reigns in the explanation. Takes a long, slow breath. "Look, I know how this sounds, but the world's destined to end."

"No shit?"

"No shit," she says. "It will end real soon."

"We talking decades? Years?"

"Weeks. Maybe even days."

"Yeah," Logan says. "That's coming up pretty fast."

He can't dredge up anything else to say. What's the play when your date predicts the apocalypse? How do you respond and stay polite? He considers the advice Donna gave him before he left, all the in-case-of-emergency scenarios for when he fucked this up. Her predictions seemed comprehensive, but they did not include doomsday prophecies while freezing to death on a chunk of argillite by the sea.

"Well," he says. "That sucks. I'd hoped this date was going okay."

"It is what it is." Stina Lorne takes Logan's hand in hers. Leans her shoulder against his side. Her presence warm and exciting against the cold wind. The closeness triggers a fresh jolt of adrenaline, sets Logan's heart pounding. He's conscious of every inhalation, senses every panicked heartbeat echoing through his chest.

"So how's it going to happen?"

"What?"

"This apocalypse. What does us in?"

"My grandfather will eat the moon." Stina closes her eyes, rests her head against his shoulder. "Well, not my grandfather, he's more the great-great-great etcetera etcetera kind of deal. My real grandfather is long dead. Cancer, right before he turned a hundred and twenty-two."

"Sounds like he did okay," Logan says.

"Yeah. I guess it's a good run."

"Sounds like great-great-great etcetera etcetera is doing okay as too."

Logan assumes that he's playing along, being part of the joke. Then Stina says: "He is. Comes with the territory, when you're an immortal wolf."

Donna will piss herself laughing about this. The moment Logan gets home and tells her, Donna will piss her pants. She'll cackle so loud their neighbours wake up, before she taunts Logan with "*I told you so.*"

"Your grandfather's a wolf?"

Stina's breath catches. "Well, *the* wolf."

"*The* wolf," Logan repeats, confused.

"You don't believe me?"

"No," he says. "It's just…"

"It's cool. I wouldn't accept this the first time, either."

"Okay."

"But…"

"But?"

"But—" Stina says the word firmly, so Logan can hear the underline. She lets the pause linger, then carries on "—My grandfather really is a wolf. He's Fenrir, the wolf begat by Loki, Wrecker of Havoc throughout the nine worlds."

Stina's eyes are still closed and her voice is low, reciting the words as a litany. "Brother of the World Serpent and Hel, Queen of the Underworld. Fettered by chains forged by the dwarves, captured by the gods at the cost of the Tyr's left hand. Harbinger of Ragnarök, when he's unfettered. Kicks off the end of everything."

She said it naturally, put it out there. Like it was no big deal.

"Wow," Logan says. "Unfettered?"

"It means he's free."

"I know what it means. Never heard it used in conversation."

"Well, I'm using it now," Stina says. "My grandfather's free and soon he'll be devouring things. He'll start with the moon, then the sun, then the sky. And when he's done, the Fimbulwinter will begin and the last twilight will overtake all."

"That's… highly specific," Logan says.

"A vague prophecy does nobody any good. Ambiguity gives people the room to insert their own message, and important shit gets lost. Some folks concentrate on the wrong thing, and next thing you get doomsday preppers and whackjobs and cults."

Logan runs through the implications. "If you're right, doomsday prep isn't such a bad call, yeah?"

"It won't help. Not with the winter that's coming, and everything that follows."

Logan says nothing, groping for words. Still half-hoping Stina's joking.

"I don't think you believe me," Stina Herne says for the second time.

Logan goes to lie, to tell her she's wrong, but the words lodge in his throat. He remembers Donna's advice, when in doubt, go with the truth. "Well, it's a lot to process, isn't it? End of the world. Disappearing moon. The woman I hoped to kiss tonight being descended from an immortal wolf."

Stina looks up at him and smiles.

"Besides, if we assume the apocalypse thing is true," Logan says, "why on earth say yes to a first date? What's the point, if we're all going to die?"

Stina's teeth are very sharp and it's very bleak up there, in the wind. "Just because the end is coming, doesn't mean we shouldn't live."

"Right." Logan swallows his nerves and says, "We should get down, yeah?"

"Not yet," Stina says. "But soon, okay?"

"The view's not that good."

"But the company is."

"Oh." The blushing warmth creeps up Logan's neck.

Stina clears her throat. "You said you planned on kissing me?"

"Hoped," Logan says. "I hoped to kiss you."

"Well, do that," Stina says. "Make hope a reality."

"Up here? We'll fall."

"That's part of the fun." Stina eases back, lying flat along the slope. Pale skin glowing in the moonlight, silver hair tugged by the wind. "Besides, it doesn't matter, right? Falling off, hurting ourselves, breaking our necks."

"Because your grandfather's coming?"

"Yes," Stina Herne says, serene and deadly certain. "This won't seem cold, soon, compared to the Fimblewinter. Best we enjoy ourselves, for as long as we can."

She waits, and he thinks she's so very like the moon, that blend of pale flesh and darkness that hides so very much. Logan shifts on the Rock, some part of him conscious of falling even as he positions himself to make out.

Logan presses his lips against Stina Herne's, the trembling warmth of her beneath him. Hears Donna's questions tumbling through his mind: *are you really going to do this? You're really willing to kiss this woman? After everything she just said?*

Yes.

Yes?

Yes.

Yes, it seems he is.

They don't fall off the Rock while making out, and Logan's grateful for that. When they don't push each other off to die on the estuary rocks, that pleases him too. He climbs down first and helps Stina back to terra firma. They return to the car, Stina's fingers entwined with his, Stina's shoulder brushing against his arm. They get into his beat-up Volvo and start the long drive home, the stereo turned down, a buzz of noise and the hiss of the tape and Logan's thoughts all about her instead of the highway. Logan doesn't think about what's coming next. He doesn't know, doesn't care. Figures it's easier to play along, fall into whatever he's falling into, regardless of where he lands.

He takes her home. They kiss goodnight. First, in the car. Again, at the door. She does not ask him in. Logan's grateful for that too. If Stina Herne suggested going in, Logan would go. He guesses he's not ready for that. Better to wait, figure this out. Enjoy the courting, as Donna says, before things starting getting real.

So, Logan drives home. Lets himself in, very quietly. Ignores Donna, in the other room, playing Xbox and drinking beer. Sneaks past and shuts his bedroom door, pulls off his sneakers and his jacket and his jeans. He crawls into bed and nestles into the covers. Logan's lips feel like they belong to someone else. He closes his eyes. Too wired to sleep.

The end of the world is coming. He repeats that idea, over and over, replays all the details: immortal wolves and Fimblewinter. E Googles, reads Wikipedia entries. Takes in all the myths and legends until his eyes are hurting. Logan wonders if he should text her, figures it's too soon.

Instead, he picks up his phone and opens the calendar. Puts a note there, for next year: *on this date, we kissed for the very first time.* Just in case Stina's wrong. Just in case he needs it, in years to come, if things turn out the way Logan's hoping. When first kisses mean less than the accretion of time. When first dates mean less than the days and the months and the years spent together afterward, but remembering the day it started feels like something you ought to do.

Just in case she's wrong, and the world keeps spinning.

Then Logan puts the phone down. He breathes in cold air and exhales.

The night is very dark. The Xbox explosions out in the lounge room seem very far away, and very unimportant. Computer games are a bad way to pass the time, if the Fimbulwinter proves to be real.

Logan shuts his eyes and remembers that kiss, and he knows there's no sleep coming.

THE PLACE BEYOND THE BRAMBLES

When last I saw you, my sweet, my love, you'd shrunk to the size of Grandma's thimble, plucked from the porch by the bees of the forest. We heard your cries, your wild shrieks of delight, as they carried you to the place beyond the southern brambles. Listened, after, to the silence that followed, to the empty fields and the dark shadows beneath the trees where no bee remained to hum its evening song.

You've been gone a five-month, and Grandma does not know your name anymore, nor does Jordy or Cousin Ferdinand or our dear, sweet Claudette. Whatever magic was used to shrink you, to make your final exit possible, stole all memories of you from those you once deemed as close as family.

But I still recall everything about you, my love, just as I remember your delighted squeal upon being taken aloft, just as I can summon the tiny hymn of joy on your lips as you fled to the place where I cannot follow. I know the contours of your face, burned into my mind on the first day we met, when you emerged from the forest in your dress of black and gold, and we conversed for hours and days on end, talked until you kissed me and declared that we would be lovers.

You tasted of honey that day, my love: so sweet; so sultry; so wild.

.   .   .

For those who prefer the technical term, you were taken by *Aspis mellifera*, the common honey bee. The Latin fascinated you, the first time you encountered it. You had me trace its genus in my books, explain the origins of the word. *Aspis:* bee. *Melli:* honey. *Ferre:* to bear. A designation proposed by Carolus Linnaeus in the eighteenth century, who later realized his mistake and tried to correct it.

In that respect, my sweet, my love, he is a smarter man than I.

People ignored his calls to use *mellificia*—maker of honey—in place of his first attempt. They did not care that it was inaccurate after growing used to the initial nomenclature. To Linnaeus disappointment, others did not fret about incorrect designations, nor comprehend the need to correct such an insignificant error.

Sometimes, in your heart, you understand things to be true, even if they are also wrong.

When we married, my sweet, my love, you carved a slice of our wedding cake and took it to the brambles. You left it there, that the bees would learn of your happiness, and spread news of it through the world.

We held our reception in the barn, danced across the dusty wooden floor and ate of the feast Cousin Ferdinand prepared, served on those great trestle tables laden with cakes and roast meats and pies. We did not own those tables, my love. Ferdinand acquired them from generous neighbors, much as he brought in the food and drink by calling upon those who owed him favors.

People thought highly of my family once, leastwise around these parts.

We had oft discussed what it must be like in the place beyond the brambles. I suspected you of being a bee-wife, right from the beginning, even though you promised otherwise. We each told Claudette different tales about the kingdom of the hives. In mine, the bees inhabited a golden land, serving the Queen with a slavish devotion. Beyond the brambles there were rivers of honey and flower-covered hills, vast swathes of clover where the bees could rejoice and play.

In your stories, the land beyond the bramble was merely another bee-hive. Bigger. Grander. More impressive. You saw no need to personify, held no truck with suggesting magic as an idyllic force in their lives.

"Why should the bees conform to your human desires?" you asked me. "Must you make strange things so familiar before you can appreciate their beauty?"

I call Claudette our daughter, but I know this child is not truly mine. No get of a bee-wife's womb will ever truly belong to their father.

Claudette shares your hair, your smile, your face. She shares your penchant for walking the fields, letting the bees gather around her. She shares your knack for speaking to the swarms, coaxing them into a conversation.

Occasionally the bees sting her, but Claudette doesn't cry out.

The bees are hers, as they'd once been yours, and I fear they will take her as well.

I am not a foolish man, my love. I knew, when we married, that it would not be forever.

The men of our village accept brides from the forest. Nettle brides and fox brides and daughters of the elm and the willow and the river. They are often beautiful, always enchanting, and none have ever stayed for long. They come, they marry, they bear us children, and then the trees reclaim them.

We do not speak of it, not in the open, but it's common knowledge such things happen. When you disappeared, oh my love, people came to our door to pay their respect. The delivered foods—frozen blocks of casserole to defrost and microwave—and said nothing about your origins.

"Be pleased you've got your daughter," they told me. "Claudette, she is a bonnie girl."

I ask about you, to prompt some lingering recollections, but their memories are fading, or faded and gone.

This, too, I expected, given my suspicions about your origins.

I make lists of the things I no longer recall: your name; our first words on the day we met; the exact and specific color of your eyes on the evening of the summer storms.

That thing you told me, that morning. The one before you went away.

I make lists of the things I remember still: we can measure the average life of a worker bee in months. Weeks sometimes, in colder climbs, where winters are long and cruel. The average lifespan of the Queen gets measured in years, often four, but sporadically longer.

I never learned your age, my love. We did not celebrate birthdays in our house.

I do not know if you're alive or dead, although I keep hoping for one or the other.

I spend the evenings on our back deck, my love, watching the brambles and the forest and the stars. I drink beer and write these letters, never quite sure where to send them, and I pretend that somewhere out there you can yet hear me and remember us as we were.

Some nights, when the sky is clear, Jordy comes out to join me. He is older—his brown skin worn to leather—and haunted by the same look that I recognize in the mirror now. He sits with me a while, and brings me a fresh beer, and the earthy scent of the field is replaced by the lilac of Jordy's hair tonic and the mint of the gum he chews.

Jordy married a fox-wife, I think. I do not recall her exactly.

"The hardest part," he tells me, "is getting used to memories that no-one else has. Treasuring them, 'cause they need to be treasured, without assuming that you've gone mad.

You loved her most, so you remember. That's the husband's burden."

And I would ask about his wife, if it would not pain him, for I've asked about her many times and I cannot keep her name straight in my head. There is something about her, as there is something about you, my love, that makes it difficult for those who weren't lovers to recall her.

Once, while very, very drunk, Jordy offered some darker advice.

"The hardest part isn't that everyone else has forgotten her," he said. "It's the dread, one day, that you'll find another man who remembers every detail."

I never asked him about this statement. I've never had the stomach. I cannot remember the woman he speaks of, so any comfort I offer is platitudes and conjecture.

But the fear of it sticks, like a knife to my gut. I can endure much, knowing I must endure it, but the thought you might have loved another wounds me beyond all measure.

I picture you there now, my sweet, my love, in the place beyond the brambles. Often I picture it, in my mind's eye, a reminder of you and where you've gone. A reminder that, yes, you are most likely happy, certainly happier than I could make you in this worn down house, on the border between the fields and the forest and the thorns.

I imagine you on a throne, my love, because I would not care to see you otherwise. This way, at least, I can pretend your departure is as much about duty as anything else. I console myself with a greater good, even if it is one I cannot understand.

I imagine you on your throne in a dress of gold and black and green, ruling your apiary subjects with kind words and a smile that soothes the soul like honey in hot tea. I picture your court with its busy rulers and its stiff, unyielding guards.

In my mind's eye, my love, my beloved, my only, I can see the rolling fields filled with clover. I can see the vast and endless hills covered in wildflowers.

. . .

This is the story I tell our daughter when she asks after her mother. You would not like it, my sweet, my love, but it comforts her more than science and truth. It comforts her more than tales of hives.

At least, it does for now.

COUNTING DOWN

Phil says he can catch a bullet, and none of us believe him.

You have to know Phil: he says shit like this. The first night I met him, he swore he could backflip from a standing start. Bet me twenty bucks, and I put up the money. He got halfway over before gravity took over and he crashed into concrete.

We called an ambulance. They hauled Phil away. We returned to our party.

I ran into him a week later, and Phil showed me the stitches, a neat row above his eyebrow, straight like the seam of a shirt.

"That's an ugly one," I said.

Phil attempted to frown and flinched. "Yeah, but it could have been worse. My head is full of bats, you know? If they'd gotten out, that would have been awful."

I said, "Better to have them free, though, instead of leaving them in there?"

Phil blinked. Then he grinned. "I like you," he said.

He gave me a twenty, fair is fair, because I'd won our bet.

And so I became Phil's friend, and learned you can't get rid of him.

. . .

The bullet thing is new. And this time, Phil's adamant, swearing black-and-blue he can snatch a shot from the air. It's not a good idea to believe him. Phil's been drinking. Hell, we're all pretty buzzed right now. When Angie holds a party, all of us fucking drink. And plenty of people will take him up on the offer to shoot him, if Phil's got a gun.

No, not *if*. I know he'll have one. Phil commits. He throws himself into things. "For real," he says, "I can totally do it. Somebody grab my Luger."

When nobody goes, he calls us all a pack of assholes and gets the damn gun himself.

Daphne says she'd be down with shooting Phil. She says it quiet, in my ear, low enough that I'm the only person who catches the words. I'm glad of that, I really am, the fact she's only willing to share that thought with me. There're many folks here who are tired of Phil's shit. All sorts of people who figure, what the hell, let the goddamn asshole get shot, you know?

People who'd take what Daphne said and use it to egg her on, put the Luger in her hand and make her take fifteen paces before pulling the trigger.

It was Phil who introduced Daphne and I. Three years back, at another party. We owe him for that. Together, it's been three years of happiness. Or, you know, as close to happy as relationships get. Phil claims it wasn't his idea. The bats told him to do it. I don't care. We owe Phil, or we owe the damn bats. They're both walking around in the same goddamn skin.

I don't want to shoot him, and I don't want Daphne to do it either. If it's Phil we owe, I want him alive. You don't repay friends with gunshots.

If its bats we owe, I want them kept inside his skull. After what I'd seen, I sure as hell don't want the bats out here.

.   .   .

You may have surmised this already, but I'd like to make it clear: Being Phil's friend isn't easy.

I know. I've been Phil's friend for six years now, and there's always shit like this going down. He used to do this trick with knives. First, he wanted to throw them at you. Told you he could do it clean, had real steady hands. No-one was stupid enough to say yes, until our friend Mandy said sure, stood against the wall and posed.

"Come on," she said. "Get it over with. Money where your mouth is, yeah?"

And Phil, he went to work. Put three knives into the plaster, all tight and snug against Mandy's arms. We started to believe his shit, a little. I mean, he was drunk, but he was pulling it off.

Then he put the forth blade into the meat of Mandy's leg, staggered over to the window and threw up in the garden.

Mandy screamed blue murder and she wasn't alone in that. Once again, we called the ambulance, but her departure put a dampener on the rest of the party.

We were all aware of Phil's presence, the threat that he might want to try his trick again if he sobered up.

Phil tells women he grew up in a circus. Says he learned this shit from his mother, a knife-thrower, and the acrobat she'd been dating through his pre-teen years. Phil lacked the passion to follow in either of their footsteps as a pro, but he developed a knack for both their arts. Picked up work as a clown for a summer job. Learned to make a crowd laugh, or at least pretend to laugh.

And I'll say this: Phil can pratfall like a motherfucker. He does it for fun, while shopping. One minute he's walking the cereal aisle, the next he's on the ground. People rush over, worry about his health.

Store managers charge in to take control, worried he'll try to sue them.

Then Phil gets up, laughing. Swearing everything is fine. "Just clumsy," he tells them. "No-one's fault but mine."

He does it because he likes the attention. The commotion and the fear, the way folks bustle around him.

Phil says it hurts sometimes, having a head full of bats. He claims he does shit 'cause he needs a distraction, a few seconds of external stimuli louder than what occurring inside his skull.

He says it's the only escape he's got, outside of a bottle of scotch.

Daphne used to say we fell in love at first shirt. Because she wore a Lou Reed *Transformer* shirt, the first night we met, and I wore a *Meat is Murder* shirt I'd stolen from my older brother. We bonded over eighties pop, after Phil introduced us. We talked, we flirted, we friended each other. It still took me three weeks to ask Daphne out, and even then Phil goaded me into it. He listened to me talk and, one day, he snapped and delivered an ultimatum.

"Throw this knife at me, motherfucker," he said. "If I catch it, you sack up and you ask her. Otherwise, you stop telling me about her, dig?"

Phil and I were sharing a flat that year. He badgered me until I gave in and threw the blade. He caught it, won the bet, and I called Daphne the next day.

Fair is fair, after all.

And that's how we ended up here.

When Phil likes a girl, he falls back on what he knows. Mostly, that's drinking, and a bunch of carnival shit. This one time, to impress a girl, he hammered a six-inch nail up his nostril. Pulled it off okay, but there were nose bleeds for two weeks after.

This one time, to impress a girl, he threatened to pull a live bat out of his ear. Gave her the whole damn spiel. "I can hear them all the time," he said. "Squeaking and flapping around in my skull."

Of the tactics, the nail worked out better for him.

And, even then, it didn't work out better by much.

• • •

This one night, a week back, I stayed at Phil's place. He was drunk; I was drunk. It seemed like a good idea. I crashed out on his couch, woke around three and stumbled to the bathroom, wondering if I would puke. Phil's voice seeped through his bedroom door.

There weren't any words in what he was saying, but there was a rhythm, like poetry, undulating and strange. It gave me an ugly feeling. I knocked on Phil's door. Checked on him, when he didn't wake.

It's February and hot as hell in Brisbane. I learned Phil slept naked, when I sat down by his bed.

The muttering stopped. Phil's eyes stayed closed, and he lay there, very still, a sheet tangled around his legs, covering his junk. When he spoke, his voice sounded very, very far away.

Phil said, "Mattie?"

Then: "Mattie, you can't be in here."

"Dude," I said. "I just wanted—"

Phil opened his eyes and looked at me. They weren't the eyes I recognized. They were dark and endless, black like polished marble. I could see things, in behind them. Bats, maybe, just flitting about.

Or, you know, not bats at all.

Nothing like bats, not really.

"You shouldn't be here," he said, real quiet, and he didn't sound like Phil anymore. I got the hell out of there, caught a cab home. Told Daphne nothing about it.

Now Phil's walking around the party, looking for volunteers. He goes past me and Daphne twice, looks me in the eyes both times. Decides and comes back to me, pushes the Luger against my chest. "Mattie," he says, "congrats. I dub thee designated shooter."

Daphne squeaks, beside me, like she's realized that he's serious.

"Phil, man, come on," I say. "We believe you. You don't have to do this."

He leans over, and he hugs me. "It's going to be okay," he

whispers. "I swear, it'll be okay."

"Phil," I say, "I really don't know."

"Come on." He glances in Daphne's direction. "You owe me. You know you owe me this much."

"Ladies and gentlemen," Phil says, every inch the showman. "Please, for your own safety, don't try this at home. And please, for the sake of your defense attorney, only help out when you're drunk."

People laugh. They're used to laughing at Phil. He's a funny guy. He turns towards me, spreads his arms wide. Takes a step back, all smiles.

Another step. Another. Fifteen paces in total.

"I'm counting back from ten," he says. "When I'm done, you shoot."

I shake my head, say nothing.

"Aim here," Phil says. Puts a finger against his temple. "Don't worry. I'll catch the bullet. Not going to hurt me at all."

He lowers his hand and takes a deep breath. Steadies himself with a nod.

"Ready?"

I'm not. I'm totally not.

"Ten." He smiles. His eyes turn black. I can see them moving inside his skull.

"Nine," he says. "Eight... seven... six..."

And me? I lift the gun.

THE THINGS YOU DO WHEN THE WAR BREAKS OUT

Your stomach does this funny lift, when they first activate the anti-grav. Nothing crazy, like you'd get if you were on a roller-coaster, but my dad, he was never a roller-coaster guy. Dad fixated on the idea the train's destined to crash, clutched the armrests with both hands and focused on his breathing to ease his nerves. Shallow breaths, in-out, in-out. Over and over for the whole thirty clicks it took to rise into low orbit.

"Dad, it's fine. We're protected," I said. "Nothing's going to happen to the train, okay?"

My father wasn't having a bar of it. "Your mum claimed that, prior to her first trip up. Perfectly safe, she said, and ever since she came back… well, you can't say it didn't affect her, eh?"

"Dad—"

He was breathing again. Ignoring me. My mother, she ventured to space early when the trains were still a new thing. She left my old man not long after she returned to earth, ran off with a bloke who worked at her office. Dad found see a connection between the two events. The rest of us couldn't. Mum claimed she could not hack it with dad, after things got rotten, and there wasn't any reason to doubt her.

Some days, I can't really hack it either. I feel ashamed, admitting that, but it remains the truth.

Still, Dad became calmer once we passed the Karman line and entered the thermosphere. You can see the dinosaurs from there, all the space-faring pterodactyls that flit toward the train like moths drawn to a light.

Dad said, "It's amazing, isn't it? Seeing them out there?"

And it was, I suppose, from his point of view. They were still extinct when he was a kid. Dad remembers the first encounter, after we ventured into space for real. They were hanging out on the dark side of the moon, waiting for us to come catch up and join them.

He always loved dinosaurs, my dad. Wanted to call me Rex, when I was born, except mum refused. She named me Henry and figured I'd turn out okay, with a sensible name like that.

Things went wrong. Of course they did. You finally take your dad into space, despite his protestations. You catch the train up— safest way to travel, everyone always says so—and you get him a good look at the creatures he loves and maybe, you think, he'll soften a bit. With luck, he'll finally stop holding onto this thing with mum and live his life a little.

So, yeah, of course, that's the day that the dinosaurs go mental, start swooping your carriage, snapping their beaks against the windows. Big noise, that. Loud as a gunshot. One crack, then another, and it brings back memories of a chick breaking free of an egg, 'cept this time they're getting in, not fighting their way out.

Thing is, it's not my dad who freaked out about it. "This is brilliant," he said. "They're like bloody magpies."

They weren't. They were big, leather-winged, and dangerous. They could survive in space, and we could not. I lapsed into the breathing thing this time, while my dad got his phone out and took a photograph.

"Dad," I said, "this is serious. They're trying to get in. They don't ordinarily—"

He shushed me, just like he did when I was a kid, speaking out of turn on a trip to a museum or library. The lights in the carriage turned red, and a polite voice informed us we should put on our seatbelts. A pterodactyl beak snapped against the glass right next to my head.

"Seatbelts," Dad said, and pointed at mine, as if I'd somehow missed the announcement. Then he twisted back to the window, cell phone in hand, and took another photo.

The polite voice returned, asking us not to worry. They planned to turn up the anti-grav, try to make a run for it.

There were dents in the side of our carriage when we disembarked at VS Station. There were soldiers in blue caps, guns slung against their hips, keeping a wary eye on the sky. One of them caught me and dad studying at the pitted marks, informed us we'd gotten lucky. "The two-fifteen out of Belfast," he said, "she's a good three hours overdue. 'Dactyls knocked her off-course, sent her drifting into irregular orbit."

We thanked him and hurried off the tarmac. Met up with my sister, who'd come out to greet us, after hearing about the attack on the news.

"Be an interesting visit," she said. "They're paying all sorts of attention about what's happening on the dark side. Nobody's mentioned evacuation yet, but it's on everyone's mind."

I sat in the back seat. My dad, up front, cycled through his photographs. He regaled my sister with enthusiastic details of the attack. "When we get home, I'll show you the pictures," he said. "Your brother was worried, silly duffer. Missed the chance to get all sorts of good shots of 'em up close."

"You were scared too, when we took off," I said.

"I," Dad said, "was apprehensive. Not the same thing at all."

They sent tanks into the dark side of the moon the following evening. My dad did not approve, but then he was an apologist. "Bloody ecological tragedy," he said. "Shouldn't be messing with their habitat like that, eh?"

My sister didn't agree.

"You're not from here," she said. "You don't really know what they're like. They're dangerous."

"Ecological tragedy," my dad repeated. He would not budge on that point. Trudged outside and taught her kids how to play Tyrannosaur. The game hadn't changed since I was a kid. He'd snarl and growl and chase them around, then fall over and go extinct when my niece pretended to be a comet.

My sister called him a stubborn old bugger. She made a fresh pot of coffee.

"How is he?" she said.

"He's good."

"No." She relinquished the coffee pot, placed both hands on the counter. "I mean, how is he, really?"

"Well, you know."

She nodded as if she truly did, and her assumption irritated me. She'd not seen my father in the flesh for the better part of a year, too distracted by her own her life to understand how poorly things progressed.

One of the soldiers came to my sister's door; a tall woman in a blue cap, blonde hair pulled into a tight, controlled bun. The soldier carried a gun slung over her left shoulder, her preferred weapons a stern, commanding tone and a sour expression. She informed us the war was not going well. Then made it clear we'd need to be ready to evacuate, if the dinosaurs advanced.

My father disappeared that evening, sneaking out after we'd gone to bed. My niece found a note on his pillow the next morning: *Heading to the dark side. Not coming back. I'm sorry.*

The soldier returned and took our report. She stressed, very clearly, no one should go after him.

We followed Dad. Of course we did. He might be going bonkers, but he was still our father. My sister called in some favors, got us let out past the city limits in this beat-up old rover. Stayed on the ground, skulked through valleys every chance we could.

Avoided open spaces, kept a wary eye out for pterodactyl's above.

"This is your fault," my sister said. "He would have been bloody content on Earth. I would have brought the kids to see him."

"You wanted him to visit," I said.

My sister's lips were a pale, tight line.

"We should have known this would happen," she said. "Dinosaurs were always going to be trouble."

"It's been fifty years," I said. "Nobody predicted this."

We fell silent, the two of us. Evacuation was due to start within six hours. If we weren't back, we stayed behind. Her wife would get the kids away, keep them safe on the trains.

Then dinosaurs found our rover, seven clicks out.

Your stomach does this funny lift, when your buggy gets attacked while you're traversing the surface of the moon. Sharp beaks rap against the thick layers of glass and you hear your sister screaming. No calm voice to explain the situation, just panic and terror and the heavy crash of your own heartbeat. Deep breaths won't relax you. If the cabin cracks, deep breaths are not really advised.

Things are going very wrong.

You think about your dad, alone on the dark side of the moon. You recall those trips to museums to study bones. You think about playing Tyrannosaur and how you squealed, as a boy, when he chased you.

You think about your mum, and how long it's been since you saw her.

You think about the crack on the windshield, getting longer. The hiss of oxygen escaping. The engine whining as you try to run, your sister screaming something about sealing the system.

You think about all the ways you could have helped your father, and didn't. The trip to the moon was supposed to improve things.

It hasn't.

And you think, *it will work out. There's got to be another chance.*

And you think, *this is amazing, look at them all out there.*
And you think, *that crack is getting bigger.*
And then you do the breathing thing. In-out. In-out.
Make use of the air remaining, in the time you've got before it runs out.

WINGED, WITH SHARP TEETH

The rain draped over Brisbane like a wet sheet, bringing a chill with every sharp gust of wind. Not the weather Steve hoped for when planning a first date, but he wasn't complaining. They huddled together in the Siam Palace on Sandgate Road, seated beneath the watchful eye of a giant golden Buddha. "A lucky statue," Duke said, patting the belly. "Bodes well, yeah?"

"Let's hope," Steve replied.

Duke ordered Pad Thai and Steve followed suit. They ate slowly, trading first date anecdotes and vital statistics. Steve learned about Duke's job as a physio out in Albion, the friendly kitchen war Duke waged against a neighbor after they both learned how to cook a perfect crème brûlée. Steve wracked his brain for interesting library stories to offer, seguing into his tale about the time he accidentally share housed with a straight dom/sub BDSM couple who possessed a lax approach to boundaries.

Despite his fears, Steve enjoyed himself. Wait staff hustled past tables, delivering drinks and plates of fragrant curry. The wind chased new patrons through the front door, candle flames dancing on every table. Their own lanky, blond waitress brought fresh beers.

Duke maneuvered himself into a position where his gaze fixed to the left of Steve's shoulder. Wet his lips, then swigged the beer, an awkward silence on its heels. Steve eased back, no sense in crowding the man. "You okay?"

Duke paused for a moment, as if unraveling the question's complexities. "So I'm going to confess something strange, given this is our first date." He glanced down and took a deep breath. "I figure it's a lot to dump on you, but life is easier when I'm upfront about it, you know? My whole deals been an issue for other guys. They don't admit it, but it has. I've *got* this weird thing, and it turns into a bigger deal over time, and...."

Oh god, Steve thought, here it comes. All he said out loud was, "Shoot."

Duke swigged his beer again, exhaled a deep breath. Steve braced himself for the worst, imagining fell possibilities.

Then Duke explained the regular visits by a flying crocodile, his expression hangdog and worried as he stumbled over his words.

Steve's relief almost escaped in a giggle, but he caught it. All in all, he'd heard worse on a first date.

After explaining, Duke blushed and focused on the lukewarm remnants of Pad Thai. Used his fork to push the remaining cashew through an obstacle course of noodles and bean sprouts, refusing to look up. Steve found his sudden flush of shyness endearing.

It seemed to Steve that tall, good-looking guys like Duke rarely needed to blush for any reason, and he relished the prospect of offering comfort and understanding. "Well..." Steve tacked a reassuring smile on the end of the pause. "I get it. Really. And I'm glad you told me."

Duke looked up from his plate, blue eyes wide and brimming with hope. Steve eased back into the canvas chair and sipped his beer, refusing to be snared in that look, not yet. "I won't tell you it will never be a thing," he said, "but I can roll with it for now. I'm cool with it. And you."

Duke fought a relieved smile and lost. Then Steve asked a question: "How often are the visits?"

Dukes swelling eagerness crested and ebbed away, his broad shoulders sagging. "Two, three nights a week."

"That many?" Steve said.

"That many."

"Ever tempted to go?"

"Nah."

"No?"

Duke pressed his lips together. A tight, inscrutable line. "As a kid, sure. Who wouldn't? Puberty hit and life got hard and man, it tempted me, you know?" He stopped and brought out a wary smile. "But as an adult? Not for ages. I don't want those kinds of adventures now. The way I see it, there's plenty of excitement here if you're looking for it."

For a moment, Steve said nothing. Then he nodded. "Okay."

"Really?"

"Sure. Doesn't sound like a deal-breaker to me."

"Cool." Duke glanced up at the Buddha and flashed a grateful smile. His teeth were short and uneven. Steve discovered that imperfection only made Duke even more fascinating.

Steve asked for a second date. Duke requested the third. They didn't truly ask, after that. Both agreed spending time together was a mutually desired state and defaulted to doing so. And so they stayed the night at Duke's apartment down on Collins Street, wordlessly agreeing it was the right moment after eating Mexican food at the restaurant down by the river.

Steve and Duke were both in love, although neither could recognize it yet. Steve worried about being too old for Duke, too skinny and overly interested in books, cups of tea, and comfort. He compounded this fear in Duke's small, one-bedroom apartment with a bicycle stored by the door. All the photographs on the walls were landscapes, taken on frequent trips overseas. The mountains of Tibet at sunrise. The dark rocks and banked snow of an Icelandic plain. Duke wrapped up in a puffy, DayGlo orange coat as he ventured across pristine arctic ice. "I don't really spend much time here," Duke said, showing Steve through. "The place is storage, mostly."

"The Museum of Duke," Steve joked, but his thoughts flashed to his own house. Three bedrooms stuffed with things. His books, and the artwork, and his fully stocked kitchen. The pantry with everything labeled and color-coded for ease of use. He said nothing and focused on kissing Duke, and their differences dropped away.

Cassie announced she was taking Steve to drinks after work, and he agreed because there was no getting out of it. They absconded to the pub round the corner, took their beers out to the garden and listened to the rumble of the trains going over the Merivale Bridge. Cassie toyed with her library ID, frustration spilling over as Steve avoided the topic of Duke.

"Right," Cassie said. "How are things with your new man?"

"They're good," Steve said.

"Just good?"

"Very good. Great, even. It's just"—Steve took a long, steady breath and exhaled—"he's being visited well into adulthood. Warned me on the first date, upfront about everything. Swears he won't leave, but..."

"You worry?"

"I worry."

Cassie frowned. "How old is Duke?"

"Old enough to make a final decision."

"Given he's an adult, and remains here despite multiple opportunities to take off, sounds like he already has," Cassie said. "Lovers don't take off because they spot an opening, Stevie. Lover's bail because they need to, or because there's no reason to stay."

Steve first encountered the crocodile on his third night sleeping in Duke's apartment.

The visit caught Steve off-guard. He'd assumed the crocodile wouldn't come while Duke entertained company. It seemed impolite, even for a winged reptile representing a magical land.

Midnight arrived and stubby legs rapped at the window,

accompanied by beating wings and an aggravated snort. Steve jumped at the noise and Duke smiled. "It's only the croc," he said.

A warm flush crept up Steve's neck, hidden but the dark. "Oh. Right.."

He'd never seen an airborne crocodile before, and Steve wasn't truly seeing one now, given his vantage point on the bed. He could hear the steady beat of wings outside and the rattle as displaced air pushed against the panes of glass. All Steve caught through the curtains were quick glimpses of detail: rough skin; sharp teeth; the long, pristine white-feathered appendages that didn't belong on any reptile. Duke slid free of Steve's embrace. "Hold on. I'll make it leave."

Steve rolled onto his side to watch. He wondered how the crocodile maintained position, jostling against the pane and scrabbling for purchase on the sill. Steve pulled back the curtains and flipped the latch, pushed the window out.

The crocodile snarled at him, a sound like the dregs of water swirling down the drain. Duke gripped the window frame with both hands. "No," he said. "Not tonight."

An urgent, questioning grunt in response. Steve flinched, seized by the impression he'd intruded on something private. Instinct urged him to run away and hide in the bathroom until they were done, but given what he and Duke shared, he fought against the impulse.

"Look," Duke said. "I've got company."

The croc met this with another growl, lower and angrier. Steve abandoned plans to move.

"No," Duke repeated, more urgently this time. He closed the window and pulled the curtains. Returned to bed and threw an arm over Steve. The steady rhythm of crocodile wings receded into the night. Steve held his breath until the sound faded.

"Sorry," Duke said.

"It's cool."

"You're sure?"

"I'm sure."

"You seem a little freaked."

Steve nestled against Duke's shoulder, planted a kiss on the stretch of bare skin. "It's fine. In fact, it's kinda sweet. No one refused a crocodile for me before."

Duke's fingers brushed against Steve's spine. "It wasn't a hard choice to make."

His lips sought the hollow of Steve's collar bone, worked their way towards the neck. Steve didn't care about the crocodile after that. He found it tough to worry about anything but Duke, during the things that followed.

There have ever been uncharted kingdoms lurking beyond the pages of an atlas. Lands who swept up ordinary people and stole them away, pressed them into service as heroes and champions. Lost boys and faithful children, brave and true and splendid; dreamers and lovers, ill-equipped for the harsh world on this side of the divide; the young, the wild, the brash, and the beautiful.

Steve brushed against those lands as a boy. A black kitten marked by a white star on its forehead stole into his room at midnight, slipping through an open window and nudging Steve awake with both forepaws. The kitten spoke in a wheezy rasp and offered Steve a grand adventure, a chance to steal away and join the Twilight Circus, have adventures with Leanna the Wild Girl as the pair traveled from world to world. Abandon his life, friends, and parents, climb outside to ride the moonbeams off to who knows where.

Steve's refusal was predicated on having tickets to see the re-release of *Star Wars* the next week, and his assumption there would be another invitation down the line. But there wasn't, not for him. The cat never returned, and Steve remained in the world of *Star Wars* and George Lucas' horrible prequels and the sequels that followed those. His days filled by school, then university, and the pleasures of the library gig, and if Steve thought about the kitten at all, it was rarely with regret.

Still, the persistence of Duke's crocodile surprised him. Steve learned to recognize its approach: the regular thump of vast wings flapping over the corrugated iron rooftops; saltwater scents lingering in its feathers; the quiet scrabble of stubby legs searching for purchase on the window sill, and the slap of its tail against the brick wall below. They'd lie in bed together, Duke and Steve entwined, waiting for the tap-tap-tap that signaled the crocodile's visit.

Duke rolled out of bed to refuse it, again and again. Declared his happiness and sent the crocodile away. Steve took some contentment from the repetition. He let himself relax.

Steve wasn't sure when, exactly, he realized Duke might say "yes," one day. They'd been together for almost a year, discussed Duke giving up his apartment. They'd confessed they loved each other, with nerves and caution to start, then with increasing confidence. They'd packed Duke's stuff and ordered a moving van, ate pizza amid the chaos of half-unpacked boxes to celebrate.

The relationship progressed with ease and order, for a time. Steve and Duke developed routines. Grew used to having each other around, sharing space, sharing ambitions, sharing everything. The doubt started with a question, maybe. Duke slipping into bed and holding Steve tight, fingers brushing against bare ribs so lightly that it tickled.

"What do you dream about?" Duke said.

"I don't remember my dreams."

"As a kid, though? What did you want to be?"

"Happy," Steve said. "And I am."

"I wanted to be Spiderman," Duke said. "That's why I refused, the first time the crocodile begged me to leave. I figured I'd get bitten by a spider, and I'd get powers here in our world instead of needing to go away."

"I dreamed of becoming a Jedi," Steve said. "But a cool one. Han Solo with a lightsaber, not Luke Skywalker."

"You'd make a good Luke."

"Not Han?

"Oh no. You'd be a shitty Han," Duke said. "But Han's a scoundrel. Short-term fun. Luke's the guy you build something with, no?"

"Oh. That's nice," Steve said. Secretly, he figured all Jedi were destined to be a shitty boyfriend. All those rules about feelings and secret loves didn't bode well for long-term happiness.

Duke fell silent and Steve listened to him breathing, placed an ear against his chest. Duke said, "Do you regret not flying away with the cat, back when you were a kid?"

"Sure," Steve said. "When life isn't going well. I get frustrated or stuck, and I daydream about what might of have been."

"Huh," Duke said.

"It means nothing," Steve said. "It's natural, thinking things would be better, somewhere that isn't here and now. But places don't fix you, and problems sneak into the suitcase."

"I dunno," Duke said. "I think it's easier to change when people don't know your history."

"Perhaps," Steve said, "but I doubt it."

"Of course he might go," Cassie said, when Steve explained his concerns. "That's always the risk with dating. Men come into your life and you love them. Most of them go away. If you have 10 relationships across your lifetime, you count yourself lucky if only 9 end with you breaking up. That's all true love is, mate. You play the odds and you find your one in ten."

"But how do you know?" Steve said. He was three beers down now, late heading home. The question gnawed at him even though Duke waited for him.

"You don't," Cassie said. "You trust him until there's a reason not too. That's how it works."

"But you said—"

"That was start-of-the-relationship advice. It's different," Cassie said. "You're mid-relationship. You've got more to lose. And he may go. That's the risk. That's always the risk. What matters now is whether the risk is worth it, and only you can judge that, yeah?"

Steve tried to take Cassie's advice and, mostly, it was easy. He and Duke were good together, most days. Good together most nights, too, but Cassie argued it was the days that mattered.

Good nights were meaningless, she said. All you needed was chemistry and hormones and a dark room, a place to fumble through the motions and figure out each other's kinks. The days were the tricky part, she argued. Managing all that time spent together, establishing mutual support. Building something the both of you valued by accepting the not-so-great parts and celebrating the parts you valued.

On their first anniversary, Steve took Duke back to Siam Palace. Duke ordered the massaman curry, and Steve the Pad Thai. Duke's curry came out hot enough that he hiccupped through the rest of the meal, and they drank wine and talked and returned home to finish celebrating.

When the crocodile came, regular as clockwork, Duke rolled out of bed. He kissed Steve on the cheek, then the lips, and he crossed over to the window. Steve thought nothing of it. He'd gotten used to the nocturnal visits. He rolled over and dozed. Not really listening.

Then: "No," Duke said. "I'm happy here."

The tone caught Steve's attention. He stopped breathing, kept his eyes screwed shut. The crocodile's tail slapped the exterior wall.

"Yes," Duke said. Then: "yes, really."

Steve exhaled. Smiled.

Then, Duke said, his voice soft as a whisper: "One day, if things change, perhaps. I don't really know. Right now… for now, I'm happy."

He came back to bed. Went to sleep.

Steve lay there, repeating Duke's words over. Perhaps. One day. Right now.

Steve took to lying awake at night. He'd listen to Duke's steady breathing, the rumble that wasn't quite a full-fledged snore. He'd study the lines of Duke's face in the moonlight. He'd wonder what it was like, where the crocodile came from. He pictured an island, and amazons, and pirates, and geese. A place where Duke would be special. Special to everyone, not just to Steve.

And, truly, that's where the fighting kicked off, even if they never said it. They would have blazing rows over the coffees Duke picked up at the cafe, or the way he'd start complaining about his job the moment he walked through the door every evening. Steve didn't have the guts to say, "I'm worried you will leave me," in case Duke turned around and said, "Good, because I will."

They weren't happy. At least, Steve assumed they weren't happy. He wasn't, but he pretended. Steve excelled at feigning happiness, given the habits built up over time.

Practice honed Steve's talent for self-deception even further as the weeks progressed, but it's hard to love someone when you're waiting for them to go. Anticipating their decision that an unfamiliar somewhere-else is an improvement on the present here-and-now. One day Steve came home early and sat in their living room, surrounded by their collective things: Steve's books and Duke's bike and the photographs of his travel.

Steve's neck ache with a dull pain that first set in right after breakfast. He needed a massage, but his skin crawled at the thought of being touched.

Steve rubbed his face with both hands. Shucked off his shoes and collected a glass of water, his socks whispering against the floorboards. The house felt different now, with someone else resided there. Better, most of the time, but as he drank Steve pondered the practicalities of living alone once more.

It's not that I hate him, Steve thought. *I'm just… tired.*

The recognition caught Steve off-guard. He placed his glasses on the counter and massaged the bridge of his nose. Last night's dishes still filled the sink, waiting for someone to accept responsibility and fill the basin with water.

Steve thought about doing them and decided against it. Content to let it slide, and confident the job would get done in time.

It still came as a surprise, when Duke elected to leave.

They'd gone through a bad week: fights about fines at the video store; fights about cleaning the toilet. Stupid fights about foolish things neither truly cared about. They'd reached détente and built a new peace, started remembering how they'd felt about each other before the fighting broke out. They talked, and they laughed occasionally. They weren't happy, or unhappy. They just stayed together and trusted in the familiar routines: dinner; laundry; work; bed. The arrival of the crocodile and its offer to leave, the whispered conversation as Duke refused.

Then, one night, Duke said, "Okay, let's do it."

Steve's eyes snapped open, in the dark of the bedroom. He let out an unsteady breath, kept perfectly still. If I move, I could stop this, he thought, and he found himself caught between inaction and panicked motion.

The window creaked as Duke pushed it wide, letting in the cool night air. Powerful jaws closed around him, gentle and firm. Duke moaned as the crocodile pulled him clear, furious wings beating upwards, driving them skywards. Steve rolled free of the sheets and scrambled for the window sill. Caught the dark silhouette of Duke and crocodile against the bright moon, receding into the distance.

Small figures. Smaller. Gone.

Steve shut the window. Returned to bed. Figured, well, that's that. We're done.

Steve embraced the relief of an ending, over that first week. No more crocodile. No more fretting, waiting for the other shoe to drop. Steve worked through the motions of daily life: got up, showered, and commuted to work. Let the machine pick up the calls from Duke's office, when they realized he wasn't coming in.

He missed Duke, sure. Pined for the little things about having someone you love in the house. Brewed coffee and watching TV on a Sunday afternoon. Conversations over dinner, texts throughout the day. The unexpected kisses and being held as you drift off to sleep.

But you can miss something and be glad it's over. Steve reminded himself of this, on the days the grief was fresh. Repeated it to friends who asked how he was doing. Embraced his role as the reasonable, coping lover-left-behind, letting people assume Duke was the bad guy. "Duke just disappeared, in the night," he'd tell people. "No note, no goodbye, no idea where he's traveling."

Steve liked that. Reasonable and coping suited him."I don't really understand how things went bad," he'd tell them. "We just... stopped working, you know? Both of us."

At night, when the bed felt empty, trying not to feel alone got so much harder that Steve cried until sleep came to claim him.

"I'm okay," he explained. "It hurts, but it's better that it happened."

Time passed and pain receded, much as Steve expected it too. In the depths of his gut Steve believed that the passage of days healed emotional wounds, even if his sadness whispered lies about the sorrow lasting forever, and there could be no feeling better given Duke left. Steve allowed those thoughts to wash over him, treated it like a tide. It would be deep and it would be shallow. Never quite gone, but often receding.

The reasonable lies he told the world consolidated into a kind of truth. He really was okay. Duke's departure was for the best.

Then, one night, he heard it: the flapping wings; the tap against the panes of glass. That faint scent of saltwater and a low, unhappy growl. Steve rolled over, pretended to ignore it. The crocodile slapped its tail against the bricks, the contact loud as a gunshot.

Steve twisted free of the blankets. Stormed to the window and jerked it open. "What?"

The crocodile reared backwards, tail swinging. It held a coffee tin in its jaws, the label peeled off and the steel pockmarked with indentations from sharp teeth. The croc dropped it into Steve's hands and grinned expectantly, hovering in place.

Steve collected his keys and levered the lid away. He shook the tin, and a letter fell out, a strand of paper with black ink on it.

Come join me, it said. *I miss you.*

Steve handed the tin back, lodged it between the crocodile's jaws. "No," he said.

The crocodile waited, expecting a different answer.

"No," Steve said, "I'm not interested."

He knew it was a lie the moment he said it. He wanted to go. Wanted it more than anything. The crocodile loitered and Steve wondered if it was grinning.

"No," he said firmly. "We tried. It didn't work."

He pulled the curtains shut and went back to bed, ignoring the wild hopes that gnawed at him.

The visits became a regular occurrence. At first, intermittent. One visit the next month, two the month after that. A new letter from Duke packed full of fresh details of his adventures. *I met the Dutches of August Peaches*, he wrote. *I learned to joust from the back of a phoenix and sail beside the Pirates of Kech.* Always, the letters ended with a plea: *Please, come; I want you; it's awesome here. I miss you.* One night, six months in, the note contained just two words: *Steve. Please.*

Steve said what he'd been saying, for weeks and months: "Possibly next time, if you come back."

The visits grew more frequent. Weekly, for a time. Then, every night. Steve grew used to the sound of wings again, the urgent rap on the window as the crocodile demanded attention.

He told Cassie about the visits. Her voice rose, just short of anger, when she advised him against leaving. "Under no bloody circumstances," she barked. "Christ, Steve, you're smarter than this."

Not the advice Steve hoped for, after confessing the situation. "I'm thinking about it," he said. "I miss him."

"Of course you bloody miss him," Cassie said. "That's what happens when people leave you. Doesn't matter how nice they were about it, missing them is part of the territory. It doesn't change the fact you shouldn't go. Running away like that, at our age? Jesus, it's outright stupid."

They did not talk about Duke after that, nor the crocodile or the things Steve hoped for. Hours later, following his most recent refusal of the crocodile, Steve closed the window and contemplated the issue in bed. The emptiness bothered him, right after Duke departed. Now Steve stretched across, making full use of the mattress. Steve wondered if he should tell the crocodile to leave for good, just accept Duke's departure and move on.

When the idea didn't sit right, Steve considered an affirmative answer. Give in and embrace the adventure, let the crocodile sweep him away.

That night, around 3:00 AM, Steve dialed Cassie's number and left a message on the machine. "What's so wrong about forgiving someone? Isn't that what love's meant to be?"

He decided and dug through the back of his closet, unearthing old jumpers and thick, neglected woolen socks. Steve shoved them into a backpack, tamped everything down and loaded more clothes on the top.

He added books, in case reading materials were scarce: his copy of *Cotillion*; the unfinished paperback of *Anna Karenina* he'd been reading for a decade. Maybe he'd finish it, if the supply of new books proved limited.

The sun set and the rain crept in with the night, sharp needles of ice-cold water that reminded Steve a raincoat may well be useful where he was going. Not that he owned one—Steve settled on being an umbrella man years ago and rarely ventured anywhere where his black brolly was inconvenient.

It would have to do. Steve positioned his pack and brolly on Duke's side of the bed and wrote an email to his boss at the library, asking for a leave of absence. He wrote a second to Cassie, saying goodbye, thanking her for being a good friend along the way.

It's not that I think you're wrong, he said, *but I wish to find out for sure.*

Steve didn't hit send when he was done. Just saved the message to drafts, in case he needed it later. He ordered Thai food, home delivered, and settled in to wait. Devoured his curry and his coconut rice and the Pad Thai he assumed would go bad in the fridge long before someone discovered his absence.

The night was cold, wet, and crazy. Fast winds and driving rain. Bad weather to drive in, let alone fly. Possibly more than a winged croc could handle. Steve perched on the edge of the bed and watched the storm rage, thought about the good times with Duke and the bad times with Duke and all the times between.

"You know this is dumb," Steve said, to nobody in particular. He just wanted to hear the words said out loud. The storm answered with rain on the roof and a flash of lightning in the distance, where it wouldn't bother anyone.

He knew that leaving was stupid. Steve didn't particularly care. He loitered by windows, searching the horizon for winged reptiles. He fantasized about seeing Duke again: what they'd say, how they'd forgive, what Duke would taste like when they kissed.

The howling wind clawed at the window, rattled the panes of glass.

Steve pressed his nose against them and peered into the distance, dreaming of who he might become when he ventured out past the horizon.

UPON DISCOVERING A GHOST IN THE FIVE STAR

At first, I considered switching laundromats.

I mean, sure, the Five Star was just two blocks from my apartment, but there's something about a ghost girl by the dryers that takes the thrill out of throwing wet laundry in, paying your money, and settling into an ugly plastic chair to wait until the job's done.

Even worse, the Five Star used to get crowded in the afternoons. If you walked in and you were the fourth person there, you'd end up using the last dryer on the left, close to the spot she haunted.

Nobody wanted that. The closer you came to the ghost girl, the weirder it seemed to be there. She'd stare at you and offer the pink balloon tied to her wrist, and your skin attempted to peel its way free and get the hell away even if the rest of you insisted on staying put.

I stayed using the Five Star because she fascinated me as much as she frightened me.

Besides, the other laundromat was a good six blocks down the road.

The ghost had been Ella Sabine once. They beat her to death, in the back of the Five Star. Three punk girls with a grudge against

Ella's older sister. All charged for the crime, but they convicted only two. The third attacker avoided prison for another decade, eventually sentenced following a second lethal beat down in Tasmania. These kinds of things make the papers. You can track the details if you desire. Most people don't. We're too used to seeing ghosts. Too used to working round them, just another daily annoyance like taxes, traffic, and those asshole friends of a friend.

The balloon piqued my interest at first. There are plenty of spirits in my patch of town, but few appear with accouterments. I'd heard rumors about the ghost of an old highwayman, down on the corner of Sycamore, who still manifests his horse and sword, and a woman out by Starling Field who holds a ghostly lantern. Both were ancient hauntings, the legacy of an era when ghosts earned more respect and fear from the living.

These days we're lucky if a ghost manifests pants to cover themselves, let alone a full ensemble and accompanying accessories. Ghosts, as with all things, are the victims of progress and the internet. We know too much about them, treat their hauntings like the tantrums of petulant toddlers thrown in a supermarket aisle. We take away the rewards that make ghostly existence bearable—attention and response.

There are more civilized ways of expressing displeasure than lingering—fueled by anger—for all eternity.

We tell ghosts this, over and over, until they look weak and blurry.

This one time, I visited the Five Star with my friend Maya and her girlfriend. I'd been telling them about the ghost girl and Maya wanted to see. Her girlfriend, Cassi Rollins, didn't appear to like Maya all that much. Cassi cracked jokes about Maya's eagerness to date other women, but they weren't really funny and never landed the way good in-jokes should. My impression, as we walked to the Five Star, suggested they'd been having problems.

It got worse, after we arrived there, 'cause Cassi goaded Maya into accepting Ella Sabine's balloon. She acknowledged it was stupid—we all knew it was stupid—but Maya did it anyway. She approached the ghost of Ella Sabine, wrapped her fingers around the length of pink ribbon. The ghost girl smiled, let go of the ribbon, and Maya pitched backwards. Fell against the cracked tile in a shuddering, tooth-grinding seizure until we dragged her out the door and into the warm sunshine.

She recovered, but Maya lapsed into uncharacteristic silence afterwards. Pale and twitchy when I caught up with her on campus, avoiding contact with her students unless absolutely required by lecture times and scheduled office hours. Weeks later, after a faculty meeting in which Maya seemed disengaged, I cornered her to ask what occurred.

"I saw how Ella died," Maya said, really quiet.

"You know how it happened?"

"No," she said. "It's like her memories took up residence in my head. I felt what she felt, lying there in pain, waiting..."

Maya shuddered and looked away. I tried to get more out of her, but she no longer wanted to talk.

Her girlfriend left a few months later. Cassi claimed she couldn't take it anymore, the way Maya closed off. I think she saw an opportunity, decided it was time.

I did not mourn Cassi's departure, but Maya disappeared a few weeks after that. They emptied her office one afternoon and announced she'd taken leave, but that was a concession to the students who'd loved Maya's classes. Nobody really knew where Maya was and whether she planned to return.

My love life, honestly, seldom involves smarter choices than Maya. I'd been seeing this guy named Oliver when the ghost girl first appeared. He used to throw his dirty laundry in with mine, but he loathed the texture of clothing dried in Ella Sabine's proximity. "My underwear's haunted again," he said. "You did it near that ghost-chick, right?"

I told him no ghost-chicks were haunting his boxers, but Oliver refused to believe me. We broke up when he started complaining about the time I spent on research. "It's the ghost-chick or me," he said, one night, and I chose Ella Sabine.

A colleague at the university did his thesis about hauntings and the cultural methods we used to disenfranchise the ghosts and disempower them. He and I ate lunch together on Tuesday, escaping our students and campus politics, and he mentioned his thesis one afternoon while we dined at the off-campus sushi place.

"It's unfair to go out there and deny ghosts their anger," he said. "Historically, the designating proper and improper behavior has been a method of control for centuries. The privileged refuse to acknowledge legitimate grievances because of tone or impolite expression. They dub people too angry, too emotional, too Other, and suddenly the way they say it means more than what's said."

"I expect things are worse for ghosts," I said. "You know, compared to the living."

My colleague didn't agree with me.

"Disenfranchise any part of society, and they'll effectively disappear," he said. "Life and death doesn't mean shit, on matters of being silenced."

I quickly changed the topic and stole one of his gyoza, but I could sense his disapproval through the rest of the meal, even after I offered to pay.

If I were braver, I would have followed Maya's lead. Gone down to the Five Star, reached out my hand. Discover what sent my friend off the deep end, made her disappear and never return. Figure out, maybe, where she's fled, so I could bring her back before the university depleted its sympathy and her job was gone for good.

Instead, I hit the internet and searched for new details about Ella Sabine's death. News reports, abandoned MySpace accounts, anything that marked her passing. There's more stuff like that than you'd think, all the detritus we leave as we live our lives.

It never seemed to help.

I came closest to reaching for the balloon just after Oliver left me. I was drunk, and I stumbled into the Five Star with a pile of laundry, a hip flask of bourbon, and a sweater to ward off the cold. Forced myself to use the last dryer on the left, although it took half the booze before I had the guts. The ghost of Ella Sabine watched me getting closer, her head tilted to the side, dark hair falling across her pale, unsmiling face. Up close, I could make out the red smear of blood staining the side of her skull. They'd smashed her temple against the dryer door, repetitive trauma until the bone cracked. That much, at least, was in the news reports when I started digging.

I loaded wet laundry into the machine and she offered me her pink balloon.

I slipped on the tiles, scrambling backwards, trying to get away.

When Oliver left me, post-ultimatum, he couldn't figure out why I'd chosen Ella Sabine.

I tried to explain it, failed miserably. But then, I fail at many things.

These days, I use the laundromat six blocks down, and it isn't by choice, not really. They closed down the Five Star, in the end. People wouldn't use the dryers, not with Ella Sabine's ghost there. Not that they ever used that excuse—we know better than to admit we're afraid around a ghost—but that was the reason, no doubt about it. I tell myself I'm not relieved, that I would have been fine to keep going back there.

I go down to the Five Star once a year, on Maya's birthday. Use a crowbar to pry open the boards up front, light a candle in a cupcake to fight back the darkness. Ella Sabine's still there, down the back, near the ancient Maytag. I sit on a plastic chair and celebrate absent friends. I sing loud and off-key—that happens when I'm drunk.

Ella Sabine is always waiting for me, full and pale as ever.

Offering me her balloon, trying to communicate what she needs with her sad, dark eyes.

One day, I swear, I'll take it. One day I'll understand her pain, what keeps her whole and strong when other ghosts fade.

I got real good at lying to myself, as the years went by.

TITHES

1.

Final stop, Gould's Antiques on Wickham Terrace. The three of them skulk in, trying to disappear amid the furniture and the ball gowns and rows of display cases. The same routine every visit: Angie slinking to the rear of the store, breathing in the scents of ancient leather jackets; Byron down by the glass-fronted cabinet, crouched so low his coat brushes the concrete floor, peering at the flintlocks and gas-masks and colonial knives; Nate just kind of wandering around, not really looking at anything except his watch, fretting about the possibility of missing their last train home.

Nate's there because they're a team. Refugees from the land of misfit toys, as Byron's so fond of calling them, students sharing a shitty fibro shack in a city that has no use for them. A motley trio against the world, the punk-girl, the goth-boy, and whatever Byron calls himself, a witch or a warlock or just strange weird.

They come to Gould's because Byron adores the place, spinning bullshit about the occult paraphernalia auctioned to secret bidders. But Nate's never seen magic here, never seen much of anything but antiques and junk. He's not even sure there's a difference between the two. Nate loathes Gould's because Brisbane's supposed to be a break, one damn day in a city where their pale and black-clad existence doesn't stand out amid the sea of tanned surfers and overweight tourists. And Gould's doesn't deliver that, not like the coffee shops and music stores and loitering by the Hungry Jacks in the mall.

Goulds is the sole place on these trips where the proprietor's judging gaze makes Nathan Heaney feel like a child playing Halloween dress-up.

The owner is an old man, squat and heavily jowled, with thinning white hair brushed back from his scalp. Despite sitting there, day after day, surrounded by the grandeur of ancient ball gowns and uniforms, he seems content with his drab cardigan and the gilded bifocals that enhance his already formidable scowl. Nate wanders down the aisle and finds himself at the counter, caught and almost trembling under the weight of the owner's stare. "So," the owner says. "Just browsing?"

He shifts from foot to foot. "No, I, uh—"

"Not a trick question, son."

Nate looks away, scanning for back-up, but the others are out of sight. "I'd like to buy something. I mean, I've got..." He thinks about his wallet, empty except for a ten dollar note. Fingers dart into his pockets, searching for any extra change. "I've got money," he pleads.

"Right." The old man picks up a newspaper, folds it. The side facing upwards contains the crossword, the white boxes half-filled with messy scrawl. Nate stands there, hands fumbling for money, face burning with shame. He forces himself to approach the counter, feigning interest, heavy boots clumping against the concrete floor. There's jewellery in the display cabinets; rings, earrings, and antiquated zippos. Old coins arranged on velvet displays, faces turned to the heavens.

Nate crouches, peering in, eyes drifting across the outmoded currency. He stops when he spots the nickel.

It's small, an interloper among the disused halfpennies, shillings, and sixpences. Nothing antique about it, just an American coin with a skull carved into the face. The silver metal buffed until each jut of bone and hollow socket is visible. Nate glances up, confirms the old man perched on his stool, scribbling words into his crossword.

Nate can't explain why he wants the nickel, why he does what he does, but he leans forward, hands pressed to the glass, and feels the door inch sideways beneath his fingertips. He lets go, breath hissing as he inhales. The world slips into freeze frame as he hovers there, expecting somebody to notice the cabinet left unlocked, but the dowdy proprietor is too far gone into his puzzle to register the skinny goth-boy crouched down and poised to shoplift.

Nate exhales, presses against the cabinet, easing the door open millimetre by millimetre. Angie squeals, sharing some joke with Byron up the rear of Gould's showroom, and the old man glances up, once, and huffs his irritation before diverting all attention to his seven letter word. Nate's hands tremble as he slides the glass pane to the left, creating a space wide enough to fit three fingers.

For a moment he hesitates. In their trio, their little team, it's never been him that's done the stealing. Angie walks off with candy bars. Byron is more ambitious. Nate is always the nervous one, too distracted, too fretful of the consequences.

And yet Nate sees the nickel sitting there—the grinning skull nestled side-by-side with the faces of dead queens and kings— and Nate calmly slips a hand inside the cabinet, claiming it for his own. It's cold and small against his palm as he nudges the glass closed, eases back like he's done nothing wrong. He tries to remember Byron's lessons: stay calm; don't rush things; wait for a distraction.

Then Angie squeals again, and there's a crash as a rack of dresses give way, and Nate slips out of Gould's while the old man huffs and puffs and shuffles off to investigate. Nate waits two blocks down, pulse hammering in his ears, until the exhilaration of the theft wears off.

Hours later, on the train home, the steady click-clack of the wheels lulling them into sleepiness, back to the Gold Coast where there's no place for antique flintlocks or ball gowns or pocket watches. Brisbane aspires to be a city, to house things laden with the burdens of history, but the Gold Coast is beaches, tanning salons, and tourists by the thousands. A city measuring its past in minutes instead of years. Nate unearths the coin and studies the carved face, puzzled by his desire to steal the damn thing. The skull seems less distinct in the murky afternoon light. The nickel, warmed by Nate's body heat, engenders an odd, unpleasant sensation like pressing a finger against an eyeball. Nate grips it, nerves taut as he feels eyes upon him, and the shadows in the carriage draw out, growing longer, deeper, and darker.

The others don't seem to notice. Not right away. Byron is staring at the window, watching his own reflection. Angie's asleep, the shaved side of her head resting on Byron's skinny shoulder, the half left to grow long hanging like a purple veil over her face. Nate knows better than to trust Angie when her eyelids are closed. Occasionally, it means Angie's sleeping, frequently it does not. He can't tell which until he eases the coin back into his pocket and Angie's eyes flick open, wide and eager. The same ecstatic grin she breaks out when she catches Nate mid illicit act.

"What's you got?" she says.

"Something I picked up." Nate hesitates, then unfurls his fingers to show her. "I think it's from the States."

Byron shrugged Angie free of his shoulder and leaned forward. "Where in hell do you pick up an American nickel in the middle of Brisbane?"

Nate curls around the coin once more. "Gould's. Five finger discount."

Angie's eyebrows rise. Bryon snorts. "No way. No way you ripped that place off."

"Cabinet was open." Nate cloaks his fist with the other hand, working his thumb back and forth along the knuckles. "You and Angie caught his attention for a minute."

Angie clicks her fingers, opens her palm to accept the coin. Reluctantly, Nate gives it up.

Byron whistles. "Jesus," he says, voice muted in respect, "you did."

"I figured they wouldn't really miss it."

"Jesus." Byron shakes his head. "Cabinet full of antique shit, and you steal a five-cent piece?"

"Maybe it's magic." Nate's grin is wolfish, eager to embarrass Byron with his own bullshit.

It doesn't work. "They don't keep that stuff on display." Byron crosses his arms, tattooed wrist peeking free of his sleeves. "You should have grabbed something cooler. Plenty of shit we could sell in that place."

"Sell where?" Nate says. "Who buys antiques on the Coast?" He sits there, sullenly waiting for Angie examination of the nickel to cease, unable to take his eyes off the coin as it twists beneath her fingers. Byron stares out the window again, face settling into a scowl. Unhappy at any sign of Nate taking initiative.

"I don't think I like it." Angie prods the coin, her expression sour. "It's cool and all, with the skull, but...."

Nate tilts his head, studying her, ready to pounce on any weakness. Angie rubs the coin's edge, frowning at the sensation. "It's weird. Not really metal, like. Creeps me out a bit."

"So I'll keep it in my room." Nate reaches out, plucks the nickel from her grip. Secures it in his pocket and glares, daring both of them to say a damn thing. Bryon snorts derisively, and Angie looks hurt.

Nate doesn't give a damn. "My score, my coin. Steal your own shit, if you've got a problem."

2.

I hate this place, Nate thinks and takes another hit of Byron's joint, a little smoke to get through the afternoon heat and oppressive summer humidity. All three of them gathered on the back steps of the house, clustered there with the dope and bottled water, enjoying the breeze that clutches at the hills-hoist and rustles the unwashed grass. Nate in his black shirt and jeans. Byron perched, stork-like, on the step above him. Angie pressed against Byron's knees, accepting the joint and inhaling a steady toke, the long hair on the left side of her scalp died pink in the two-and-a-half weeks since Brisbane.

Nothing real happens on the Gold Coast. Nothing but summer and rain and the heat that turns their fibro rental slick and humid as a sauna. The neighbor's cat clambers over the fence to their left, a streak of gray fur disappearing into the long grass. Nate tracks the jaunty, tingling bell on its collar as the moggy crosses the yard. The journey halts three feet shy of the other boundary, the cat hidden in the two-foot grass and weeds. Hesitant to approach the shadow cast by a tall fence of sagging timber slats and rotting hardwood beams.

Nate refuses to linger on that particular shadow, and he doesn't blame the cat for sharing his caution. Ever since Nate stole the coin he's been cautious about dark places—hallways, ditches, the leeward side of buildings. Ordinary shadows seem too deep, too long. No longer trustworthy.

"Jesus," Byron says, "I'll almost be glad when uni starts again. At least the classes have air-conditioning."

Angie nods, breathing against the joint, the same agreement they've made every time one of them makes that complaint. Nate grunts, bored with the exchange, digs through his pocket in search of the nickel, sorting through the pocket shrapnel. Finds the familiar, unpleasant touch of the nickel with his fingertip, warm and dank as a mangrove floor. He runs his nail across the surface, tracing the contours of the skull.

"We should go to the movies," Angie says, reeling off another plan for the sake of filling the empty spaces in their conversation. "Go catch a stupid flick, get out of the heat."

And again there's agreement, silent and universal. But they're all broke: too broke to go out, too broke for anything but smoking their last joint. *Jesus*, Nate thinks, and he slips the coin out of his pocket, wrapping its warmth in his left fist without knowing why.

"Hey," Angie says. "What the hell's that?"

They follow her finger, searching the fence-line for God knows what. Byron slouches to his feet, seeking a better vantage point. His eyes are bloodshot and his shirt hangs open, tattoos of ankhs and pentagrams inked along his ribs.

"Can't see nothing," he says, and Angie jabs her finger.

"Next to the second missing slat," she says, "down by the clump of dandelions."

Nate sees it: a twitch in the overgrown weeds, a silky flicker of darkness. He tightens his grip on the nickel and the motion halts. But now they can all discern its presence. Sense it without perceiving, like the shadows have evolved into a living phenomenon, hunkering in the overgrown grass. Something that watches, a tangible threat, and everyone's struck by this emptiness that's cold and terrible and forlorn as a lost soul. Angie, at least, starts shaking.

"Let's go inside," Nate says, and he knows Byron is nodding. Byron who's already standing but not willing to look away. Then the darkness, the emptiness they're looking at without really seeing, congeals and spreads through the overgrown weeds, creeping forward like a rising tide. Nate wills to shadows to stop, but the coin doesn't obey him. He panics and pockets the coin in case they have to run, letting it drop amid the pocket change he carries around to camouflage its presence.

The shadows halt their advance and panic melts away, all of them breathing slow and moving slower.

"Jesus." Angie's shaking, wild eyes searching the fence. She edges back towards the house, clutching at the old stair rail. "Nate, that was you. What the hell did you do?"

"Me? Not a thing." Nate collects the dropped joint, rescuing it from the rotting step.

"Bull," Angie says. "You had the nickel out again, yeah?"

"I don't got it on me," Nate lies.

"Fuck off." Byron's voice is shaky, but the threat is there. He grabbed at Nate's wrist, pulling at the closed hand. "You've carried that thing everywhere since Gould's man. Don't pull this shit."

Nate turns to Byron, stares him down. For the first time, Byron sees danger in Nate. He releases the arm and steps back. "Jesus, Nate. What the hell?"

It's hard not to thrill at the fear Nate senses, the acknowledgement he carries more than a pilfered five-cent coin. "Back off, both of you," he says.

"Nate, it's doing something," Angie says. "Your fucking coin's summoning that thing, making it go away."

"Like magic?" There's nothing friendly in the way Nate says it anymore, and a small part of him hates the loathing in his tone.

"Yeah." Angie's voice stretches around the word, weak and reedy. "Yeah, exactly like magic."

"Christ, Angie, you're fucking stoned."

"She's not," Byron says. "No more than you and I are."

"It's just a damn coin."

Angie pulls herself to full height, gets into Nate's face. "You claiming you didn't notice that?"

"Notice what? There's nothing there." Nate screws his eyes shut, holding back the irritation. He wants to lash out, shove Angie away. Buy himself a little space, find somewhere cool and well-lit to contemplate the coin and figure this out. Instead, Nate takes a deep breath before meeting Angie's stare. "I'm suggesting you might see things things that aren't there. You know, again. Like last time."

"Fuck you," Angie runs her hand across the stubbled half of her scalp, fingertips teasing the longer strands at the edge of her undercut. "Fuck you, Nate, for trying to gaslight me on this shit. Fuck you very much."

She retreats, preferring the sweat-box heat of their house than sharing the steps with him. Nate watches her departure with his mouth clamped shut, fighting the urge to shout that he's sorry, to give in just like he always does whenever Angie doesn't get her way. Byron looms by the door a moment longer, shaking his head in disgust. Then he disappears to comfort Angie, leaves Nate out there alone with the joint, the brewing storm, the shadow, and the nickel Nate no longer dares to touch.

They spend four days avoiding one another, brokering a terse detente. Nate promises himself the nickel stays in a drawer, but never seems to follow through. He reaches for the coin without noticing, always tasting the same cold terror and the quickening pulse. He tries to leave the coin alone and discovers that he can't, that he'll pick it up and fondle the metal until the unseen presence musters the shadows and begins a slow advance. Nate smokes endless cigarettes to cover his nerves, prowling the house like a caged beast.

"This isn't fair," Nate argues, cornering Byron in the kitchen. "She can't expect me to take her seriously, right?"

Byron doesn't turn away from the counter, attention focused on spooning instant coffee into a chipped and dirty mug. "She's scared, Nate. Something weird happened. Has been happening since you got the nickel."

"That doesn't mean it's magic."

"We both saw something."

"We all saw something," Nate says. "I don't think the nickel's the cause. It's… I don't know… an illusion or some shit. A natural phenomenon. A coincidence."

"That's three things." Byron's voice is steady and even. He picks up the kettle and pours, stirs three times and removes the teaspoon. Byron sips while staring out the kitchen window, scanning the fence and the long grass.

"You got a real explanation?"

"I don't," Nate says. "You're our resident conjuror of cheap tricks, By. I mean, shit, the amount of crap you've spewed—"

"Nate." His name stated with gentle calm, cutting him off mid-rant. Byron turns to study Nate, dark eyes wary and expecting trouble. "Nate," he says, "what's up? Why's it so important this be unconnected to the coin?"

"'Cause it isn't. Magic ain't real, man. It's an alloy, copper and nickel. Stamped metal scratched up for a creepy art project. No big deal."

"Maybe," Byron says, "but now it's more to Ang, right now. It's more to me. And I think you recognize that. You're right there with the two of us. Your nickel's doing weird shit, Nate, and it worries me and Angie. What we saw, it wasn't normal."

"We saw nothing," Nate repeats.

"Felt then, fine, if the nomenclature matters. The result's the same." Byron turns to his coffee, fills the kettle and sets it to boil. "I can find us people who'll help. Hell, I'll find people who'll take it off our hands, pay a little money and deal with the weird shit it brings."

A small part of Nate sees the sense of the plan, but pride won't let him acknowledge it. Nate reaches for the coin and stares Byron down, forces the taller man to look away. "You come after my coin, and there will be trouble."

"Okay." Byron turns all attention to the whistling kettle. Pouring, stirring, adding milk. Leaves Nate to look on, frustrated and angry.

"All that shit you used to tell us about Gould's selling occult shit, that was just talk," he says. "None of us took you seriously. Not me, not Angie. You know that, right?"

"Your prerogative," Byron says. "Doesn't change the fact I know people."

Later, hours later, Nate walks up to Angie's door. He calls her name, not shouting it, but forcefully. Coaxes her out with the promise he just wants to talk, unrelenting until Angie opens up and blocks the doorway to her cluttered, clothes-filled room.

"Well?" she says, hands on hips, her jaw set and ready in case Nate lapses into asshole behavior. Every inch a woman looking for a fight, except for the wounded fear in her eyes.

"I'm sorry," Nate says. "Really sorry. I didn't mean to imply you were, you know…"

"You saw it, Nate. Admit it."

"I saw something." Nate leans against the mold-tarnished wall and wishes it wasn't so damn hot in the house. "But I don't think it's the nickel, Ang. You're freaking yourself out with the idea, and…"

"And what?" Angie reaches for the door, ready to slam it shut.

"And nothing," Nate lies, trying to block the memory of eyes upon him, the nightmares he has every night. "Nothing happens with the shadows. It's just a coin, yeah? A little freaky lookin', kinda cool, but just a cheap antique."

For a moment he thinks she buys it, 'cause she doesn't close the door in his face. Lies have always been Nate's talent, the thing he brings to the house. Angie leads, Byron does. Nate creates the half-truths that allow them to stay friends.

"Show me," Angie says. "Get the coin out, here. Prove its nothing to do with the creepy thing."

For a second Nate hesitates, 'cause he can feel the coin through his jeans, warm and getting warmer. Eager for a moment in the light, exposed to the bright world. Nate's instincts warn him not to do it, that the lie is over once she sees that the shadows are becoming stronger, omni-present.

But the coin wants out and Nate obeys. He rummages his pocket and produces the nickel, opens his hand to display it to the world. The shadows in Angie's room congeal faster and thicker than those in the yard, the dim fluorescent bulb doing far less to slow their pace than the golden afternoon light.

"Fuck, Nate," Angie says, voice soft with fear. "Just put it away, okay?"

Nate works to close his fingers, but they refuse to cooperate. Trembling, fighting back, ligaments and tendons straining. The shadows reach forward to envelop Angie, stretching like the wings of some great bird. She tries to run but Nate is in the way, blocking the easy path out. The shadows grab her, engulf her, bulging and swelling as she struggles. Angie screams, but the shrill fear is very distant, as if she's in another house instead of an arms-length away.

Through it all Nate can't close his fingers, can't lock the coin in a tight fist or fling it away in desperation. Angie's screaming grows even fainter, so faint it's almost lost and gone within the swirling darkness.

Then Byron arrives, slapping at Nate's hand. Wrenching back fingers and forcing the coin to drop free, clattering against the hardwood floor. The shadows retreat, and the grip on Nate's hand stays clamped down. "What happened?" Byron shouts. "Nate, where's Angie?"

Nate points to the center of Angie's room, where the shadows are thinning and receding to their usual place. Where Angie lies amid the puddle of her dirty clothes, cold and pale and scarcely breathing—still as corpse waiting for its funeral shroud.

• • •

Angie lies in the hospital bed, all wires and tubes and sallow skin. The room beeps, beeps, beeps, marking heartbeats and hissing breathes, reminding Nate the machines are doing part of the work that keeps Angie alive. Nate hates this place. Sand-colored walls, sand-colored curtains; another fucking permeation on the endless beige the Gold Coast embraces.

"Hey," Nate says. "Hey."

He's holding the nickel, has it coiled tight in his fist, thumb tracing the ridges cut into the side. He wants to give it to her, to tuck it into her fist for luck, to do whatever magic it can to help her out. But the coin is moist, unpleasant to hold, and he knows in his gut it'll make things worse. He reaches out with his other hand, places it over Angie's still fingers. She's smaller, tucked into her hospital bed, but Nate prepared for that. Hospitals reduce people, shrink them down to nothing before easing their passage from this world.

"Hey," he says, "just, don't die, okay? Hold on a bit. Hold on. Byron's got a plan."

Nate kisses Angie's forehead, just in case it helps. Angie sleeps on, breathing and beeping and hissing away, and Nate knows the shadows stalk her still, predatory and eager to take their revenge on the woman who identified them. Nate senses the lurking emptiness he first detected in their backyard, on the train. He clenches the nickel in a tight fist and wills the shadows back, but they remain. A permanent watcher, waiting to pounce.

Byron waits out in the hall, cigarette in hand. Unlit, but toying with the cancer stick to fight back nerves, trading furtive glances with nurses convinced he's about to spark up. When Nate approaches, Byron stares with glistening eyes, fighting back tears.

"We're getting rid of your fucking coin," he says.

Nate bites his bottom lip and tightens his grip. "It's just a coin," he says. Damned if he knows why. Another untruth he can't help himself speaking, even if his brain knows its wrong.

"That's bullshit, and you know it," Byron says. "I'll make making the fucking call."

And he disappears down the hallway, cigarette still in hand, heading for the bank of payphones only used by pensioners and deros. Nate stands there, watching him go, unwilling to open his hand. He's afraid that letting go will free the thing that watches him, let it retreat into the room and savage the sleeping Angie. He's terrified that maybe what Byron's saying is true, and that everything that's happened is all his fault.

3.

Byron lines up a meeting for three in the morning. Wakes Nate and drags him to the narrow parking lot tucked beside Australia Fair, the big mall a looming shape behind them as Byron pulls in. Australia Fair is close to water, like everything on the Coast, nestled next to the highway that runs parallel with the beach. Beyond that is the estuary where the Southport River meets Pacific. The dodgy end of the Coast, home to junkies, students, and the ill. Informal camping grounds for the homeless come sundown.

Nate waits beneath the streetlight, nickel in his pocket, wondering if someone will show, if Byron is serious when he claims he knows people, and why they have to meet in the middle of the fucking night. "You certain we're making the right call?" he asks, again.

Byron's frown is all the answer Nate needs: angry and nervous at the same time. "I've been thinking," Byron says, "about you and the coin. You stealing from Gould's without getting busted. I figure they let you lift it. I think they recognized the coin was trouble and wanted it gone and you were the patsy who fell for the set-up."

"Maybe," Nate says, because he doesn't want to agree, because he still wants to pretend that there's nothing wrong. "You never mentioned who we're meeting out here."

"This guy's a friend of a friend." Byron searches his jacket for a cigarette, casting furtive glances down the street. It's dark there, in the mall's shadow, and the soft tick of the streetlights seems loud and alien in silence. "Not someone I know, but he's probably, you know…"

"Dangerous?"

"Maybe. Obviously not above board. Definitely not white magic."

They realize too late that they aren't alone. "And what constitutes white magic, fuckhead?"

The figure walking down the car park ramp is one of the biggest men Nate's ever seen. Six-five, broad-shouldered, head shaved down to gray stubble. His dark suit blends seamlessly into the gloom of the night and there's a short, stubby weapon in his right hand. Not a gun, not quite, but its shape is close enough. "So," the big man says, "which of you has the coin?"

"That depends," Byron says. "You Sabbath?"

The big man snorts his amusement. "Sabbath doesn't make house calls, mate. He sends me."

Byron chews over the information, not sure how to play it. Nate's eyes twitch back and forth between the stranger's weapon and the cheerful grin. He makes the circuit three times before Byron digs deep, finds the courage to say, "You got a name?"

"Randall." It doesn't suit him. The feral, misshapen beauty to Randall's face deserves a better match. A name to suit the predator's smile and the unsettling fire behind the eyes. Nate's putting some thought into running, but Byron isn't ready to surrender. Nate watches his friend adopt a grin, stepping forward to meet their visitor.

"I'm Byron. He's—"

The big man, Randall, fires his weapon. Two darts thump into Byron's chest, the steady click of electric current breaking the still of night. Byran slumps to the ground, limbs doing the stun gun fandango.

Nate backs away. "What the hell?"

"Taser," Randall says. "You've bonded with the coin. You decide what needs deciding. I didn't want this munter getting in your head."

"The coin—"

"The nickel." Randall makes a tiny O with his thumb and forefinger. "Little thing, skull, ugly as sin. You have it, right? I'd hate to reload and go through this again."

"I've got it." Nate drops a hand to his pocket, but Randall darts forward to catch his wrist. Strong fingers wrapping around thin bone and flesh, twisting it up and away and around behind, locking the arm behind Nate's back and torquing ligament.

"None of that, mate," Randall offers the threat casually, confident of Nate's obedience. "No touching it, not out here. Trust me, better for all concerned. You got that?"

Nate forces an unsteady nod against the pain.

"I want it said aloud, mate."

"I've got it," Nate says. "No touching the coin."

Randall lets him go, delivers a gentle shove. Nate stumbles, concrete kissing his knees. A fresh, bright spark of pain. "I don't get it," Nate says. "It's just some weird-ass nickel."

"Lots of peculiar things in this world. This one's a long way from home." Randall produces a cigarette and cups both hands around the tip, flame blossoming between his palms. "Can't say we're fond of it, me and Mister Sabbath. Too bloody disruptive, you know?"

Bryon stirs, coughing, whimpering like an injured animal. Randall takes a short step, builds momentum for a kick that catches Byron in the teeth. Nate flinches, looks away. Fights the urge to reach for the nickel and let the shadows eat this asshole. "That's—"

Randall coils around, a predator eager to pounce. The words die in Nate's throat, stick there until he coughs them free and forces speech through the knot of fear. "Beating my friend's not exactly going to convince me to… you know… deal."

Randall smiles, transferring his cigarette to his left hand. "Look at the stones on you," he says. "Good for you, kid. Good for you."

Nate exhales, and Randall's fist lashes out, buries deep in Nathan's stomach. He folds over, gasping for air, and Randall takes hold of Nate's hair.

"Now stop being a fucking idiot, yeah? I'm not here to negotiate with you. That coin, it's all kinds of bad news. One curse if it's stolen, another if it's given away. More effort than I'm willing to put in, mate, all things considered."

Nate coughs, splutters, forces himself to breathe. "Then… what?"

"What do I want?" Randall lifts the cigarette to his lips,

breathes with casual ease. "I'll help return the nickel to the original owners. You want rid of it, they want it back. Seems straightforward enough, yeah?"

No, Nate thinks, *not easy at all*, but what comes out of his mouth is a small, reluctant, "Yeah, I guess."

"Good call."

Randall takes off across the highway. Long, easy strides carrying him away from Nate and the sucking, unpleasant sound of Byron trying to breathe through his wrecked lips and teeth. Nate hesitates, just a moment, hand hovering over his pocket, but Randall calls out and he moves, jogging over empty lanes to catch up. He follows the big man down to the riverside park, along the pebble paths no-one but the homeless use wit any regularity.

"Whatever you do," Randall's voice floats back through the darkness, "don't throw a ciggy into the water. Damn shit'll go up in flames if you give it half a chance."

Nate's already wheezing with the effort of keeping pace, staying close enough to see the vague shape of Randall's silhouette in the shadowy night. He can barely think of smoking, think of anything but the coin, the big man leading him into the darkness, and the prickly points of fear digging their tines into his intestinal tract. He's so focused on it all that it catches him by surprise when Randall stops, settling down on his heels, and lights a small candle.

"We're here." Randall nods at the path, the tightly packed pebblecrete leaving the shoreline and winding towards the highway underpass, a pedestrian convenience no-ones bothered to use in all Nate's years on the Coast.

There were urban myths about the tunnel, local tales about rape and murder and worse, stories that may be bullshit for all Nate really knows. But standing there, next to Randall, with the flickering candle lighting up the concrete mouth and the urine scent in the air, Nate can't help but acknowledge that there's something wrong, some aspect of the open gullet and the darkness inside that appears too thick to be real, obscuring the far end just forty or fifty meters away where Nate knows, instinctively, he should see the glow of a streetlight.

Randall kneels down, sets the candle on a patch of grass, using his body to shield it from the wind. Nate stands by, arms slack at his side, legs hollowed out with a fear he can no longer explain. He advances with four uncertain steps, positions himself by Randall's elbow. The big man's scent is two packs a day and very cheap cologne and, faintly, hints of both sugar and sulfur.

"This here," Randall says, "it's very do-not-try-this-at-home, yeah? You'll wake up tomorrow, your sheila'll be on the mend, and we all pretend like none of this happened. You understand what I'm saying, mate?"

Nate offers a mute nod.

"Out loud," Randall says.

"Yes. I understand."

"Great. Exactly what I need to hear." Randall gestures to the underpass. "Move your arse, get close to the tunnel as you can, and place the coin on the fucking ground. Once that's accomplished, you're done. You bail out before anything else happens, right?"

Another mute nod, this one met with a stare, and it takes Nate a few seconds to realize he should move instead of saying yes. He ventures towards the tunnel mouth, leading the way with the fist holding the nickel tight. He blinks, trying to get his vision to adjust, to penetrate the uncanny darkness. There should be neon lights to guide him, or moonlight at the far end. Instead, the depths of the underpass are ink-dark, an endless void stretching into infinity. No matter how his pupils dilate there's no peering through.

"In and out, kid," Randall says, voice pitched low so only Nate can hear. "Don't fuck around."

Nate nods and takes a few more steps forward, but that's as far as he gets before he sees something: a kind of thickening in the darkness. Frost-touched air flows out of the underpass like an exhalation and the sudden bite of it makes Nate open his hand, the nickel dropping and bouncing on the pebble path, rolling towards the tunnel mouth.

For a moment Nate watches it go, mutely processing what just happened, then he kneels and reaches for the lost coin, dimly aware of Randall shouting *something*, angry words Nate can't make out.

As he stretches, fingers straining, the darkness congeals into a long and twisting tendril that slithers free of the tunnel and curves around the coin. Nate freezes, kneeling, reaching forward. A desperate thought about fighting the writhing tendril flits across the mask of terror. Then a second tendril slides clear of the gloom, advancing on Nate with the sinuous, winding inevitability he associates with snakes. Nate reaches for the coin, and the tendril wraps around him, and pain ignites every nerve in his wrist.

Randall is there, grabbing Nate by the shoulder and hauling him free, tossing him back and out of reach. "None of that, mate. Mister Sabbath made you a deal, we're returning your fucking hobo nickel. Leave the poor bastard alone, yeah? He's only the messenger."

For a moment the tendrils hesitate, poised in front of the big man. Randall shows no interest in giving ground, no interest in anything but staring down whatever exists in the shadows of the tunnel.

And Nate, he sees the nickel going, watches it being dragged into the shadow. The part of him that doesn't want to let it go makes one last desperate dive and reaches for it, crossing the tunnel's threshold, plunging into the darkness beyond.

For a moment, the moment before he screams, Nate marvels that what he feels creeping up his wrist isn't cold, not for all the ways it bites and numbs and chills him down to the marrow. No, not cold at all. But it's the only word he has for it; a frost that emerges to fill the absence, blighting heart and soul. That's all he gets time to think before the pain obliterates all conscious recognition and Nate's scream really opens up.

Later, when he comes to, Randall is standing over him, cigarette in hand. Nate blinks and stares at the shaved scalp, the little point of orange light that is the burning cherry. Randall leans down, forces one of Nate's eyelids open, waves the hand-rolled cigarette back and forth, watching the pupils. "You'll do," he says. "Better get up."

Nate doesn't want to obey, but he does it anyway, levers himself into a seated position. They're back in the car park, in the shadow of Australia Fair. Nate's hand strapped to his front with strips of white fabric. Bryon's leaning against the fence, shirt missing, hands pressed to his nose. There's blood splattered down his pale, skinny chest, and he doesn't look in Nate's direction.

"Just so you know," Randall says, "you truly are a stupid fucker."

He offers a hand and lugs Nate upright with casual ease. "Could have gone smoothly, if you let the coin go, mate. It would have cost you a little less."

Nate stands there, nodding, taking it all in. He tries moving his fingers on the bandaged hand, fails. "I can't feel anything," he says.

"Like I said, mate, stupid." Randall exhales, drops his cigarette on the concrete. "Collect your friend and get your arse to a hospital, let the doctor take a squiz. Won't do shit, most likely, but you never know."

"And if they can't help?"

"Get some practice using your other hand, 'cause that one's fucked for good."

Nate opens his mouth to argue, then shuts it when he catches the warning look in Randall's eye. There's a rage burning there, behind the pleasant facade. Nate can't place what gives it away, but it scares him. Terrifies him like the darkness in the tunnel, the unseen thing that emerged to track the coin.

"So, all this?" Randall gestures between them. "Never met, yeah? Mister Sabbath will not hear from you, or that dipshit, ever fucking again. Whatever occurred down there, it was just a bad dream. Agreed?"

Nate says nothing and Randall steps forward. Steps and looms, a big man with the ability to inflict harm, and part of Nate wonders that he can yet muster fear of physical harm, get that quickening of the pulse at a clenched fist and the promise of violence.

He chooses not to test it. "Agreed," Nate says. "A bad dream."

"Good call. Now fuck off, mate. Check in on your girl. See if she's doing better now the bad voodoo's gone back home where it belongs."

Nate fixes a stare on the big man, honing in on the glimmer of red light in Randall's pupils. "And she'll be okay, right? Angie, she'll be better?"

"Sure, kid. That's the deal." Randall pulls out the pack of cigarettes, taps a new one free, and plants it in his mouth. He holds Nate's stare the entire way, as if daring him to call the bluff. "We're done, you understand me?"

Nate nods, once. "We're done."

He turns and walks, leaving Randall and Bryon both, stalking into the night that smells of saltwater and petrol fumes and the faint scent of brimstone. As Nate makes his way along the block, heading for the mall and the streets beyond, the path that'll lead him to the hospital, he's careful to move from streetlight to streetlight, spending as little time as possible walking through the dark.

Nate catches Randall's laugh behind him, a soft chuckle tinged with respect. He counts the seconds until Byron does the math, realizes he's left behind as Nate skulks off. That Randall is still dangerously close, the same big man who tasered Byron and showed no compunctions about hurting him.

There's sixteen seconds before Nate hears Byron call, a quick sprint down the footpath path. Nate keeps walking, moving forward, sticking to the light.

THE MINOTAURS & THE SIGNAL GHOSTS

Once upon a time, well back in the day, the Minotaurs weren't so small a threat as the gang you see today. Instead, they were big and bad as hell, and they ran with a guy, Horns, who got himself grafted in a big-city clinic on his mother's credit. Not a smart dude, all things considered, but he wasn't no-one to mess with, and the Minotaur's done good under his leadership, good enough to claim all the blocks by the river, everything right up ta the bridge where the Lizards' turf begins.

Now some of that goes to the Minotaurs, sure, on account of them recruiting 'em big, mean, and ready to fight, but some of comes down to Horns' work too. He's a hefty guy, and tough as hell, and he doesn't shy away when it's time to make a mess of some other fella's guts. An' it ain't long before he's feared, and the Minotaurs intimidate the other gangs right along with him.

Now in those days the Signal Ghosts weren't like you think either. They were smaller and secret, the kind of gang that picked out the runts of the litter, and they didn't bother with any of the streets on the surface 'cause they spent all their time mapping the wreckage of the railway tunnels. Nobody really gave them two minutes thought, and when we did, we figured they were chickenshit, or weirdo's who feared the sun, so we let 'em keep the underground and fought for the places that mattered.

Only one day Horns isn't happy knowing there's someone

out there who doesn't piss themselves when they hear his name, so Horns gets together a posse and takes his boys into the dark, following the old D line, leadin' this expeditionary force that's more like a small army when you start payin' attention. They follow the tracks until they find an old station the Ghosts are using as a crib, all secure and well-lit and shined up real nice. And Horns thinks, yeah, this place ain't bad, so he walks out into the middle of platform and calls out their leader to introduce himself, all official-like. "Time to clear out your people," he says, all knuckles and snarls and unsubtle threats. "The tunnels near the river are Minotaur turf. You got two hours scarper 'fore we break heads and do this the hard way, dig?"

"Whatever you say," the head Signal Ghost says, all calm and pretty as you please, and he leads his people deeper in, following the tracks and the signals through the wreckage of the subways.

Horns is right chuffed about the way it all goes, congratulating himself for playing it cool and forcing the Signal Ghosts to back down. He's perched in the splendor that once belonged to the Ghosts, feeling like a big man. He tells his boys to go nuts on the place, so the Minotaurs piss in the fountain and tag the walls, making a real mess of everything the Ghosts built. And after a while it ain't fun no more, so they go a little deeper, seeing what's there, and when they push their way through the rubble-filled tunnels, they find themselves another station the Ghosts have done up right nice, all painted and shiny and equipped with generators to keep the lights running.

"Well shoot," Horns says, "this is much nicer than what we got," and so he walks out into the middle of the Ghosts again and makes his new demands. "Two hours to get out or we're breaking heads," he says, and once again the Signal Ghosts leave their home behind.

Only this time the Minotaur's ain't so happy about their digs, especially once they're done with the pissing and the tagging. They're deeper underground, for starters, and the tunnels aren't easy to get through. An' the old station stairs leading up the surface got broken during the quake, so everyone has to climb using ropes and raw muscle. Even Horns ain't pleased to be there, getting reports about the noises coming out of the deeper shafts, but he's proud and dumb and unwilling to show fear, so he tells his boys they're staying put and sets himself up a throne, and since Horns ain't exactly the kind of guy who listens to complaints, the best the Minotaurs can do is grumble and moan and bitch.

An' then the rumors start about the new place the Ghosts have set up, a big lair right out in the middle of the big ol' Central exchange, the king-daddy station that makes the rest look tiny, and Horns starts thinking and fretting about the Ghosts having something that they Minotaurs don't, about how bad it will look if word gets out they're living large after the Minotaurs ran 'em off. So he gathers his boys and he selects himself a posse, and together they head into the deep tunnels, the ones worst-hit during the quake, where only the Signal Ghosts really know what's what.

And it ain't easy for the Minotaurs to go that deep, not like it is for the Ghosts. The Minotaurs picked their boys for muscle, brought in the biggest and the strongest to join up and fight, an' the Ghosts were always thin and small, the kind of boys who could squeeze through the rubble of the wrecked tunnels. All the Minotaurs know it's a rotten call, but that don't stop Horns at all and none of his boys are willing to complain, so they stumble through the dark and scrape through narrow gaps, losing skin and gaining bruises every step of the way.

An' then they hit intersections, branching shafts that go off to the left and the right, or points where there's even more choices, places where it's easy to lose your bearings. Tunnels where a wall fell down or a sewer main broke, whole sections that get flooded and force the Minotaurs to retrace their steps.

And it's round then that the Ghosts pick the Minotaurs off, throwing knives and rocks from hiding places, disappearing fast once they've bloodied someone up. The dark don't bother them none, see, 'cause the Ghosts got used to the murky black, and the tunnels don't bother them none, either, 'cause the Ghosts are small and know their way and slide through the narrow gaps all pretty as you please. An' sure, the Minotaurs get one or two, torture 'em plenty to get the secrets and find a way out, but you can't follow a Ghost down there 'cause they disappear 'round a corner and never come back, an' you can't stay put 'cause the other Ghosts come to distract you and your prisoner disappears while you're trying to stop your boys from bleeding.

So Horns' crew aren't happy about this development, and one of them finally gets the guts to mention it to their leader, and Horns shouts down their complaints like it's no big thing. "They're just a bunch of skinny Ghosts," he says, his nostrils all flared with anger, "weedy little punks with rusty knives who live in caves that smell of piss. Anything they do, we can do, yeah?"

An' he keeps his crew moving, going further and further in, and every time he turns around, Horns finds he ain't got as many boys as he remembered startin' out. An' even this don't stop him, so he continues looking for the Ghost's Grand Central, 'til even Horns can't ignore the fact that he's hungry and tired and sick of the dark. He tries to turn his posse back, finding their way to the surface, an' the Ghosts keep hitting 'em 'til there ain't none but Horns left walking.

An' it's hard for Horns to feel big and tough, walking through the murk all on his own, especially when he can hear the wet slap of Signal Ghost feet echoing through the tunnels. An' for a while he convinces himself there's nothing worse, listening to his enemies follow him through dark, but it turns out he's plenty wrong 'bout that too, 'cause eventually the Ghosts stop following him and leave him all alone, just a big strong Minotaur 'banger wandering through the old subways, lost in the twisted mess and wishing he could figure a way home.

An' they say he's down there still, living on rats and sewer water, trying to find his way out, but I don't think the Ghosts have that kind of mercy and Horns' never had that kind of smarts. 'Cause it's a smart man who chooses not to fight a Ghost on its own turf, and the Minotaurs learned that the hard way, way back in the day.

HORNETS ATTACK YOUR BEST FRIEND VICTOR AND OTHER THINGS WE CALLED THE BAND

Selby showed up for the lecture with pink hair.

I sat behind her, ignoring the professor droning on about Deleuze and rhizomes and hypertext. There were thirty-two students in Contemporary Issues in the Arts, maybe twenty of them who bothered showing up. I recognized the other regulars now, the folks who attended class every week. I didn't get along with them, more often than not. Nobody except Selby proved interesting.

On the break, ducking out to grab vending machine coffee, I tapped Selby's shoulder. "Your hair. It's new?"

I cringed the moment the idiotic question left my mouth, but Selby chose not to hold my awkwardness against me. "Yeah, did it yesterday," she said. "My brother helped with the color."

"Big change, but I dig it."

A clumsy gambit. Not because I thought my opinion mattered, just trying to keep a conversation going. A fumbling gesture towards a friendship built on something other than sharing a lecture.

Selby wore sunglasses and a grubby gray shirt that morning, her cuffs streaked with paint and ink. The sunglasses meant she nursed a hung over, surviving on Red Bull and stubbornness. I fed three dollars into the machine, punched the buttons for white and two sugars. The internal mechanisms gurgled, then pissed a stream of dirty liquid into a paper cup. If you squinted, you could pretend it approximated coffee.

I drank it because a bad caffeine hit is better than nothing, at that hour.

Selby wasn't really with it that morning. Her turn came to feed the machine and Selby glared at the Nescafe logo instead, holding up the queue. I grabbed her arm, yanked her aside before Della Kingston, lined up behind us, lost her cool and started bellowing.

"Listen," I said, "you doing okay?"

"I caught this band on the weekend." Selby took off the sunglasses and rubbed her bloodshot eyes. "They're local. And good. And… shit, trust me, yeah? You gotta check them out."

"All this because of a gig?" I glanced at her hair again, putting the clues together. People had been having epiphanies all semester, figuring out who they were. Pink dye jobs appeared out of nowhere, as did piercing and tattoos. We all made bad decisions throughout that first year of university life.

"You don't understand, P." Selby jabbed my arm with her sunnies. "They aren't just a band, okay? They changed my fucking life."

"If they're that good," I said, "how come I've never heard of them?"

"Well." Selby put the sunglasses back on. "You know what we're all like with hometown boys?"

And really, that explained it. Nobody truly believed real art got made on the goddamned Gold Coast. I'd spent my first semester figuring out ways to leave the city for good, go start my real career in a place with more to offer than beaches and tourism jobs.

"A great, life-changing local band." I tried the idea out for size, but the doubt crept into my voice.

"Trust me." Selby studied me from behind her dark lenses, her expression inscrutable. "Wanna come, the next time they play?"

To my surprise, I did. Curiosity drove my interest: Selby

struck me as practical and focused. Too driven for pink hair and a revamped look because a band's music changed her life. I wanted to understand how and why it happened.

Figure out what made this band worth such a radical transformation, and whether they'd do the same to me.

A week later, at the Playroom, this skuzzy bar on the shore of the Tallebudgera River where live gigs were a regular thing. The band didn't seem like much, coming out. Another rock-and-roll four-piece: guitar, drums, and bass, with a singer out the front.

The bass player, short and feral, with torn fishnets and bronze eye-shadow. The singer, tall and lean as hunger, with crimson nails and a dirty fringe that hung over his eyes. They kind of group that wore their influences on their sleeve: a bit of David Bowie, a whole lot of Cobain.

It was nineteen ninety-eight, and their vibe seemed overdone.

Selby grabbed my arm, dragged me up to the front. I followed with reluctance and a glass of bourbon, stuck with her because… well, I was eighteen.

I was eighteen and Selby was Selby. My curiosity encompassed more than the band.

Still, they didn't seem like much, gathered up there with shabby instruments. Selby guessed my first impression. "Wait," she said. "Let them play. You'll see."

The band didn't speak to the crowd, really. The drummer shouted "two-three-four," and they lurched into a snarling opening chord. And then I saw. Oh shit, I saw. And Selby was fucking right.

I didn't remember the song, only what happened when they played. The moment the whole band… well, lit up. Shone with this hideous, coruscating color straight out of a Fusceli nightmare, streaked through with writhing strands that might have been emerald or crimson or sapphire, if only those words were accessible. I couldn't do it. I doubt anyone had it in them. The weave, hypnotic as a kaleidoscope, undulating and wholly alive. No way you could look away and divert mental resources to a task as petty and small as sourcing the perfect word to describe the spectacle.

I don't remember the songs, but twenty-one-years on that light is still with me. I stood there, slack-jawed, right by Selby. There was no other choice but staring. The light didn't give you any. It shimmered and weaved in time with the music, drawing every eye in the Playroom towards the foursome on stage. The rest of the world grew dark, fell away. Shadows lengthened as the band's radiance bloomed, growing brighter with each blistering squall of guitar, drums, and lyrics.

I don't recall how long the played, but I remember when they ground to a halt. Spots danced in front of my eyes, and Selby clutched my arm. Her voice suffused with urgency. "You understand now, right?"

"Yeah," I said. "I totally get it."

The next step became figuring out exactly what I'd got.

Hours later, when I was at home and in bed, I wondered how they'd done it. The Playroom had a lighting rig, but it didn't have the chops for a show that wild. Their design focused on illuminating the stage, making punk bands and metal-heads visible while they played.

The question gnawed at me, ate away my capacity for sleep. I'd enrolled with a double-major: journalism and art. One to please my parents, the other so I could live with myself. But I made a shitty journalist. Lacked the drive to keep pushing through the surface details, the interview nous that led to engaging questions and unrehearsed answers.

A good reporter needs a will to ferret out why things are happening, uncovering truths and bringing them to the public. The only truth I wanted to dig for, the only thing I truly cared about, involved the band and their glorious light.

The singer didn't talk to the audience. Never introduced himself or the rest of the band, no friendly banter between songs. They were a blank slate we could project upon, and a mystery to solve.

Selby and me, we hatched plans to figure out their identity. It seemed the proactive option.

Selby got a job at the Dog House in Broadbeach. Hooked up with the guy who scheduled the acts for the club and badgered him for details: who did he talk to, when he wanted to book the group? Who gave him the name and poster designs? Answers were never forthcoming, but it didn't stop her trying.

I coaxed my way into freelance gigs with the local street press and bluffed my editor into running a series about live music venues around the city. It furnished me with an excuse to poke at the Playroom and the Hard Rock, even that pub on the highway stretch of Robina where the band played an early gig.

The bookers proved an ineffective resource. Never remembered who they'd brought in to play, nor where they'd first encountered them. Every story featured the same three movements: the band appeared, rocked, and took their leave. Lugged their gear back to the van and drove the hell away.

They were a band who gave you nothing, not even a proper name. The first time I caught them, they were Luster Fatale. The second gig, Whisky-Whisky-111. Then Hornet's Attack Your Best Friend Victor. Then All That Glitters, then Sabretooth, then another name entirely. They never used the same details twice, always performed as a new entity. It should have been confusing, but we all recognized they were coming. The fans would stumble across a poster and lock onto the details without knowing why. It sparked a shock of recognition, deep in your stomach, heedless of the band name or whatever face they'd plastered up.

This one guy, Skinny D, dubbed the mystery a cheap gimmick, akin to their steadfast refusal to speak to the audience. The rest of us agreed Skinny D was a prick. Despite his loud protest of overrated gimmickry, he'd still loiter by the bar at gigs, desperate to see the band come on, eager to bathe in their glow.

As fans, we loved the mystery, even as we tried to solve it. In fact, we believed the secrecy was necessary to their appeal; if they became too prominent, too easily found, they wouldn't be ours anymore. We were certain they'd lose their powers, that whatever made them shine would dim, or go away, the moment too many eyes were upon them.

We argued about the way they achieved it, given their stripped-back approach. Some called it a trick done with smoke and mirrors. Some claimed they weren't precisely human, and they lit up because they were aliens with extraordinary powers. Skinny D offered this theory involving a collective synaesthesia, transforming sound into an oscillating melange of brilliant crimson, sapphire, and emerald.

They were psychic, he said, and that's what made them great. They played with our minds to make it happen.

Nobody believed him, really, but our explanations were no better. It didn't matter how many gigs you saw; the band remained a mystery.

Selby lived with her parents throughout her first year of uni. During the second twelve months she battled with her mum—an ongoing feud about the band and her degree that boiled over in mid-March and continued until December. Selby moved in with her brother after she got kicked out. I came round to help her move, loaded crates of CDs and cassettes into the trunk of my beat-up Ford. She sat on the front step of her mother's house, smoking. "I hate it here," she said. "If it weren't for them, I'd leave today."

Selby's hair was pale green that week. She'd shaved the left side of her skull. I knew who she was talking about, why she stayed. We both knew. We were fans.

"They have bands in other cities," I told her.

"Not like ours."

"You don't... you can't be sure of that. I mean, how could we know? It's not like anyone here is making noise, or raving to folks in Melbourne about what's going on. Maybe this happens everywhere, and nobody talks about it."

Selby didn't seem convinced and I couldn't blame her. We both knew the pattern after new fans encountered the band. The period where they wondered if they were the only one to see the lights, where they kept dragging people along to confirm the light existed, let them know they weren't going mad or caught in a bad trip.

That fervor didn't last, nor did the evangelism. What replaced it was fear, and this nagging unease about the things you remembered: the light and this slurry of noise, all sonorous and angry and barbed with half-formed lyrics. Random words, sometimes, that hit you like a brick to the side of the skull and lodged there, permanently, as you blinked the spots away.

When the first rush of evangelism passed, you kept the band to yourself for a stretch. Then you started talking, and the secret mutated into a thing we all shared, something more real than surf and sand and the bars full of tourists that echoed through the night. A fraternity of people bonded by this mysterious group, always alert for the next gig. Sustained by the hope we'd be there when the band finally made sense. When everything about them unfolded like an origami bird, a beautiful object wrought from the ordinary paper using artistry and skill.

It's why we all kept our mouths shut when people started dying. We hoped, ordinary as we were, there remained some capacity to transmute our lives into something glorious.

At first, the deaths were background noise. A situation we acknowledged when forced to, but never mentioned among ourselves.

In 2000 there were rumors they'd cut an LP, a limited release intended for the local stores. The records were disks of amber vinyl, the sleeves a riotous mess of abstract color and shape. We flocked to music stores, hoping for confirmation, but when they unearthed nothing, the rumor mill launched into overdrive, buzzing about a treasure hunt. Then the LPs showed up in weird-ass locations. You'd see a record hidden among the boogie-boards at the local K-mart, or used as placemats in the Yum-Cha restaurant off the Broadbeach mall. Fans negotiating with managers in a frenzy, wheedling attempts to purchase their spoils, or they shoplifted the vinyl with varying degrees of skill and hoped for the best as they ran. Skinny D got arrested trying to steal from the Southport charity shop, but it turned out all he boosted was The Cars' Greatest Hits LP, tucked into the wrong sleeve.

This period exposed the band to folks outside its limited fanbase. A Bulletin reporter interviewed Skinny D, tracked down the rest of us for comments. Selby went on the record. "This city's idea of art is longboards sculpted from stainless steel," she said. "Worse, it's <censored> sandcastles done en masse on the beach. Surely we need a space for mystery. Mystery and <censored> entertainment for someone other than tourists and bogans."

The reporter made a big deal about the intensity of Selby's stare. Included pointed details about her hair, now styled in a two-tone mix of crimson and electric blue, and the steel hoops put through her eyebrow. At no point was drug use suggested, but the implications were definitely there. Subtext as subtle as a length of clue-by-four: look at these crazy kids, seeing weird shit while stoned.

We tried to boot-leg the bands shows for a while, after the LPs came out. Turns out you couldn't record their music, couldn't get anything but the crowd noise and the drummer's initial count. The moment you heard "three, four," the whole damn audience fell silent. All that remained was tape hiss until the gig concluded.

Being a fan got weird after Selby's brother died. Rick discovered the band a few weeks after her, tagged along and exposed himself to the light and the mystery of it all. Fell down the rabbit hole just like Selby, just like me, just like everyone. Skipped shifts at McDonalds to see them play, started obsessing over the idea that he might miss a gig.

Rick passed early. One of the first wave, before we realized it was only happening to fans. No logical cause of death, according to the coroner. Rick came home from the Tugun Hotel show and flaked out on the couch. Then he didn't wake up for two days, and Selby realized he was gone.

Her parents buried Rick in the lawn cemetery up near the university, this bland stretch of grass with gum trees around the perimeter. The dead marked with marble plaques that broke up the flat expanse of sward. Not long after, Selby dropped out of her degree and transferred into Law. Not giving up art entirely, merely treating it like a side gig. "I've learned what I need to. I'll never be great. Time to earn some money, yeah?"

As the death toll climbed, my editor called and quizzed me about my knowledge of the band. Did I associate with any of the deceased? Could I leverage any connections to get us fresh details? His eyes set on writing a feature, using it to land a job with a paper that dealt in news instead of trumped-up blog posts about local shows and new albums.

"You've got insight, yeah? You're part of the scene?" He salivated, already dreaming about what the access I could give him, the story that might be there. "You understand why all this happens, right? Why people keep going to their gigs?"

I told him to go fuck himself, and my days as a journalist ended before they'd ever truly begun.

I visited Selby and her family in Canberra, last Easter. Her husband invited me, wanted her old friends nearby. I slept in a spare room with a single bed and some of her art hanging on the wall. She'd developed a minimalist style after leaving the Gold Coast in her rearview. Squares of white canvas with a few carefully placed black lines. Lots of right angles. Very ordered. Very stark. Selby kept it up, the painting and sculpture, even after she worked at a firm. Still created, years later, when she realized she and her law career were no longer compatible.

One night, after her kids were sleeping, Selby confided that she still felt guilty about her brother's death.

I tried to comfort her and failed. "We warned him. We told him the gigs were getting ugly."

Selby's attention stayed focused on her fireplace, the merry flames dancing across the fake log inside. They were yellow and orange and red, chaotic and wild like all fires are.

"Warnings didn't help," she said. "We all knew it was dangerous; it's what made them real. That's why everyone kept going, after we should have stopped."

The truth of it robbed me of any argument, and Selby quit talking about it. We sat and listened to the crackle of the fire, the dancing flames and glowing embers desperate to escape the grate.

Then, Selby offered to make a pot of tea and we talked about her husband while the leaves steeped. Edgar worked as a surveyor for the Department of Main Roads, spent his twenties listening to Beatles albums, Springsteen and Bob Dylan.

I swore to stop attending gigs. We all did, once or twice.

They were playing at The Doghouse, in Broadbeach, this weird bar with a stage and open space. High ceilings, like a cathedral, which meant it took forever for the cigarette smoke to permeate the room. They served three-dollar bourbons until ten o'clock, but fans weren't drinking hard enough to get drunk by that point. It was the night they played under the name T-Rex 69. Selby was there, and Skinny D. Rick was still alive too, although he wouldn't last much longer. The band rocked and the swirl of color appeared, but this time it glistened like sunlight on an oil stain.

Nobody danced. Not that kind of gig. We stood in place, staring, letting it all wash over us. Then someone went down, scratching at their skin as if wasps nested in their pores, and the band kept playing, droning steadily on as the panic seeped through the crowd.

The fear wasn't unusual anymore. It started happening earlier that year, right after the articles came out. I knew fans who were getting stoned or shooting up before the gig, drugging themselves to stay mellow as the light hit the audience.

Failing to turn up proved unconscionable. We knew fear, but that wasn't the worst part. Like whitewater rafting and heroin chic, the fear of death makes unpalatable things exciting so long as you figure you'll come through it safe and the toll will get paid by other guys.

No. the worst part came after the gig, when you returned home feeling hollow. The dark and ordinary days that followed, tinged with a hollowness that left you craving something. Food, drugs, alcohol, pain—all were fair game. Things to tide us over until another show satiated the empty void.

. . .

So I tried to quit the band. We all did, at one point, and it was often idle talk. I made noise about needing to step away for two straight years before I attempted it. Truly meant it every time I uttered the claim, but then I'd see a poster for a new gig and realize it was theirs, and the pull was too strong to deny.

Selby quit them for good the year after she graduated. She was halfway through her first contract with a firm, doing paperwork and wondering if law was a mistake. But she decided the band no longer fit her world and left them in her past.

She'd stopped dying her hair by this point. She took the rings out of her eyebrow before heading into the office. We collectively called this period The Time When Things Hit the Fan and Splattered. I was finally scheduled to graduate, two years later than I should have.

It would be another eighteen months before I could make quitting stick.

I know of fourteen deaths attributed to the band. I expect the actual death toll is much higher, as my personal circle of friends includes only a handful of the hundreds of fans that regularly attended shows.

And this number doesn't include the punters who got proactive. Besides the fourteen "unexplained" deaths, I know of at least a dozen suicides, kids who swam into the ocean with a gut full of pills and let themselves get carried away by the tides. Kids who hung themselves from balcony rails on the seventh floor of the Marriott. Kids who visited the cliffs in Burleigh State Park, just up-river from the place I first saw the band's light, and took a swan dive into the rocks below.

I expect there are more deaths we could link to the band, if only someone bothered to poke at the details around the final days of the bands devotes. Every adult carries old wounds from their younger, dumber years. Our scars were deeper, and our regrets stronger. The thing we loved became a slice of hell, destined to kill us if we didn't do the job ourselves.

. . .

I wasn't at their final gig. They played it under the name We Will Always Have the Lighthouse My Melancholy Bride. No overt signs it would be the end, but we all knew they were over. One last show to say goodbye, then everyone was free.

They weren't playing clubs anymore, not in the conventional sense. They'd set up in The Co-op above a fish shop in Southport, played this little room built for poets who performed at candle-lit open mic nights. I visited the space a few weeks after it went down. I stood next to the make-shift bar at the rear, positioned under a liquor license that was twelve months expired. Traffic noise floated up the stairwell, mingling with the smell of deep-fried batter and thick-cut fries. You'd be lucky to fit a hundred punters in, and those punters would need to get friendly.

I sat on the Co-op's sticky floorboards and produced a tiny Walkman, slipped in a boot-leg Skinny D made of the final gig. It started quiet: the analog hiss, a cough, the muted hubbub of the crowd. Then came the hush as the band picked up their instruments, a faint click as the singer adjusted his microphone stand.

The drummer shouted and clicked his sticks together: "Two-three-four."

And after, the stretch of empty tape. Nothing to hear until the first body thumps into the floorboards about fifteen minutes in, followed by others a few minutes after, a whole audience collapsing and gouging themselves, ripping away until they drew blood.

Nobodyknows what happened to the band that night, but the fans were still there a few hours later, comatose and half-alive, when the guys who ran The Co-op came by to lock up. They called paramedics, and then the cops. The last gig made the six o'clock news, and the band was a public menace.

I heard all the stories from Skinny D, when he dropped off the tape. He stood on my front step and sneered around his unlit cigarette. "We missed a fucking awesome show," he said. "Best they've done in years. Never going to see their like again."

I told him I wasn't interested. That me and the band were over.

"That's your problem, P," Skinny said. "You give up on things that matter."

He caught a plane to Melbourne a week after that. Said he couldn't handle living on the Coast anymore, that he'd stayed this long for the bands gigs and now the gigs were over.

Skinny D fell asleep mid flight and never woke up. No cause of death ever released, but it wasn't hard to figure out.

Selby moved away two years after her brother died. It took me longer, sure, but I fled the city too. Felt pride in escaping, getting out alive.

I dropped out of university three weeks prior to my final exam. Landed a public service job two states over, dressed in a long-sleeve shirts and ties. Days spent shuffling papers around a desk until it was quitting time. I stayed there for fifteen years, until a new government came in and downsized, cutting jobs like they were the ballast that weighed everything down.

There were protests about the cuts, an angry demand that public services needed public funding. Liberals raging at the conservatives. My friends versus the enemy. I wanted no part in that, so I took my severance package and flew home for a while. Figured I'd see what'd changed since the Coast and I parted ways.

There wasn't much that seemed familiar, beyond the beaches and tourist straps. The council tore down the Playroom, used the lot for a park by the river. The Doghouse, also gone. Transformed into a Chinese restaurant that served sub-par honey chicken. The Co-op where the last show took place didn't survive a second year. They board avoided legal trouble in the final gig's wake, but couldn't bring in enough clientele to maintain the budget after. People claimed there were ghosts, or talked shit about disrespecting the victims who'd died there.

The terminology amused me. Victims, like those assholes weren't fans who would crawl over broken glass to be at that final performance. All punters who attended knowing death was rather likely, embracing it as part of the deal.

I stood down on the beach and dialed Selby's number. "There's nothing," I said. "The Gold Coast won. There's literally nothing left anymore."

She told me one of her kids was sick. That she'd call me back in an hour.

"Sure," I said. "Talk to you then." And I hung up, knowing she wouldn't call. An hour turned into three real easy. A sick kid became an all night problem. Returning calls slipped off the to-do list and parenting took over.

That's how it goes when your friends spawn tiny humans. We were middle-aged now, Selby and I. Fading away, because we missed the chance to burn out with the other fans. Making do with the choices still available, pretending those decisions we'd already made didn't nag us like an old wound that hurts before a storm.

I've been drinking. You should know that. The hour is late and I am very drunk, sitting here in a Southport bar two blocks from my motel. I'm thirty-eight and unemployed. I'm thinking about Selby more often than I should, picturing her at home with her daughters and her husband. Selby, with crows' feet at the corner of her eyes. Selby, with that sad, quiet way she talks these days, and the art she does on Thursday afternoons, and her habit of going silent and careful when I ask her how she's doing.

Tomorrow I fly back to the real world. Head back to the apartment I can no longer afford, the life no longer governed by the demand I be in the office by nine. Tonight, I drink and remember: the band; the light; the friends we lost. The people we used to be, with hopes and dreams left unfulfilled. I drink to the goddamn memories, and then I have another.

A list of things I regret, looking back: not having any real talent for art, nor the dedication to be outstanding through hard work and training; not working harder at the street press job, building it into a career that meant something; not keeping the mohawk I got at twenty-three, leaving it as a statement that I no longer wanted to fit with the world.

I regret that's no longer an option now. That a man my age getting a fresh mohawk draws assumptions he spent the weekend at a shitty costume party and took his punk outfit a little too far.

I regret so much in my stupid life. Not telling Selby how much she meant to me, how sorry I was when her brother passed away.

And I regret not being there for that final gig. I regret missing that last chance to see them shine, being part of the exodus. I regret not figuring out how they did it. I regret not pushing harder, trying to figure that out.

The bartender delivers another glass of Merlot. She's young, early twenties, hair pinned up like she's got time-travel plans involving fifties greasers later. She smiles at me, shy. Maybe a little wary. I'm drunk, and I've been tipping big. Wary is smarter, right now.

I get her attention before she turns away. "Hey. If a guy wanted to catch some live music in this city…"

"Yeah?"

Her tone makes it clear: definitely nervous about the old bloke asking questions that might be flirting. "Not like that" I hold by hands up, try to walk back the implications I might hit on her. "I'm new in town. Just need recommendations. Somewhere to go. Tonight."

She looks me over, and God, I feel old. So bloody old and so bloody useless. She says, "What kind of music do you like?"

"I'm not fussed, so long as they're live and good."

She gives me a place and an unfamiliar name. Say's they'll be onstage around 10.

And I hold my breath, hoping… shit, I'm praying that I'll get that feeling again, that little thrill of recognition when it's one of their gigs.

But it's not. It's just this band she knows, friends of hers who play locally and do all right. I thank her and follow her suggestion. Spend the next three hours at the rear of a shitty hipster bar, hating young men with ironic beards and the young woman who lean against them. I drink. I get drunk. I walk back to my crappy motel, trudging from streetlight to streetlight.

The street is wet and cold and windy. There are headlights, in the distance, coming over the bridge between Southport and Surfers. They fly past, and then another. Young guys doing seventy in beat-up cars, not paying too much attention. I stop and watch them come.

The headlights are bright and pure. More rushing up so fast. God, I think. God. It would be so easy.

A fifth car hisses by doing twenty over the limit. The tail lights fade and the night grows dark again. The clouds ease their way into becoming a real storm, flecks of water hitting my skin. It's cold, but it's not cold enough.

There's no real choice but to keep walking.

EIGHT MINUTES OF USABLE DAYLIGHT

1.

My friend Katie left Brisbane a decade ago, no longer content to live in the darkness. She applied for a green card and paid the bribes, moved to Pennsylvania where the sun still rises in the East and disappears behind the Western horizon. Her emails wax rhapsodic about the uneven, unpredictable rhythm of it all. "It's glorious, Mika," she says. "I'd forgotten how warm sunlight is. There's people with suntans, and they grow crops in fields."

After she moved, Katie found work in a distilling operation, one of the smaller companies. Sometimes she sends me gifts she's nicked from their supply: bottles of distilled sunlight, transmuted into a heady golden liquid and sealed with cork and wax. Smuggled past the sniffer dogs and customs agents, delivered to my flat by the ne'er-do-well friend of a ne'er-do-well friend. The dark glass warm and pure and pleasant to touch, engendering smiles as they're cradled in your arms.

Her latest delivery arrived in the false bottom of a plastic crate, hidden beneath a layer of dashboard dolls with hula skirts, hibiscus flowers, and a sucker where their feet should be. I hide the product in my safe, put a hula girl above my dash. Her hips do a shimmy when I fire up the engine, keep shaking as I pull out into the empty street. I drive down to the Seven-Eleven and treat myself to a Coke, for I am now in possession of five hundred milliliters of liquid daylight.

I get to work, a spring in my step. It will be a good week. A good month, if I am smart.

2.

There has been no daylight in Brisbane for five years, a hundred and twenty-three days, fifteen hours, and thirty-six minutes. The first months were hard, all of us confused and alone in the dark. The confusion didn't last. We picked up and got on with life. Trusted in the government to throw resources at the problem, figured out ways to make do while they tested solutions.

The news remained bleak despite all that. Some parts of the world went dark and stayed dark. Some remained touched by daylight. Science provided no way of explaining the situation, which meant there was no discernable means of fixing it. Distillation proved the only means of bringing the sunshine in from the few, scant regions where the sun yet shone.

We adapted to our situation, once it became clear no solutions were forthcoming. These days Brisbane's streetlights switch on at 8:00 AM, an artificial daybreak we take for granted. They turn off twelve hours later, nightfall, another demarcation we maintain out of habit. Hydroponic grow houses ensure we're all fed, albeit with limited fare. UV lamps and vitamin D shots ensure that our biology continues to function. They tag all daylight brought in through regular channels; the supply monitored and regulated to verify we use wisely it.

My ritual, with my illicit delivery, has been honed over several years. I start my rounds near lights on, when the yearning for daybreak is strongest. The filthy rich have already fled the city, heading for brighter places, but there are still plenty of those with money and no desire to leave. I deal to the eccentric, the well compensated, and the extremely well off and idle. Men and women in fake tans, wearing linen and gold jewelery. Or quiet, observant people who long for the days when open-air gardens existed without a spiderweb of lamps clustered overhead.

I move through the check-points, alert my regulars there's

product available through the use of codes and ciphers. Start the bidding, let it build. Ten bucks a millimeter. Twelve. Thirteen. We're coming up on fifteen dollars a mil before Midday arrives, and it'll be higher still by the time the day's done.

I receive a call from my sister, Pavio. I do not answer, for I am hustling, and she does not leave a message for fear I will get caught.

Pavio's always feared the consequences of what might happen, if I'm busted, and I cannot say she's incorrect to harbor those concerns.

3.

At six, I head to West End and drop in to see Lillian. She runs a café off Boundary Road, just through a peeling doorway set in the red brick wall. Years ago, before the darkness began, they sold the finest latte I'd ever tasted. Now authentic coffee costs sixty bucks a shot, and most of us show up there because Lillian makes good tofu scramble and does her best with chicory flavored drink we're happy to accept as a coffee substitute. I prefer Lillian's fake imitation because she doesn't pretend. It's listed on her blackboard as Hot Nostalgia, the chicory cultivated in her own private grow-house three blocks over, supplemented by a smaller crop of arabica trees.

I don't conduct business in Lillian's café because her uncle works for the police. He commands check-points and riot squads, the jackboots designed to keep order, and for all that Lillian is not her uncle the connection bothers me. The sole time I broke this rule, back when I first started dealing, it was a harbinger for a close call with the authorities. They raided my apartment, cops and military personnel rummaging through my possessions.

Only luck saved me from being arrested—I'd sold the last of my product earlier that morning. Had they come four hours prior, I would have been a dead man walking.

Lillian and I didn't speak for three weeks after the raid went down. When I came back, I played it safe: kept our conversation general, steered clear of questions she might have about my business.

Still, I like to see her. I couldn't stay away. Lillian scrambles tofu as I claim a seat, and pours me a Hot Nostalgia. Serves it with the vague contempt baristas hold for drinks that are not truly coffee. Her eyes are very large, very gray. The light seems to dance in them when my glance meets hers. Lillian smiles, and I smile with her, even after all these years.

She says, "Pavio stopped by earlier, wanted to track you down."

I dig my fork into the scramble. I know what Pavio wants from me, but I do not discuss business with Lillian. Caution is my watchword now, for all that I think of her as a friend.

"I told her you've been dropping by around dinner," Lillian says.

When I do not answer that either, she changes the topic to a mutual acquaintance whose applied to immigrate, like Katie, to the lights of Pennsylvania. Lillian tells it as if this were news. As if everyone didn't apply for a green card these days, looking to get away from the streetlights and the loneliness that comes from spending your life in darkness.

4.

I finish eating and contemplate a cup of actual, honest-to-God coffee. Tell myself I can afford it, once the daylight sells. Lillian sees me hesitate, knows what it means. We edge as close as we will get to an admission that I'm dealing: "Good week?" she says.

"Not yet, but it's coming."

I'm staring at the menu board and Lillian smiles.

"You can owe me," she says. "Fix me up later, yeah?"

I agree in a moment of weakness. My simple, cardinal rule: it is smarter to work in cash than trade in endless credit, better to owe people nothing instead of fretting about the debt. I break that guideline on rare occasions, but the aroma of real coffee, dark and bitter, wipes out my practical side.

I sit by the counter, take my time. Sip with slow, deliberate languor, savoring the flavor. Lillian cleans her ancient machine, dumping grounds from the portafilter with a look of resignation.

It's hot in the cramped quarters, amid the tight press of tables and the close-set walls. She wipes perspiration from her forehead, grabs my dinner plate, and transfers it to the tiny kitchen out back.

I wish it wasn't like this, but it is. She is who she is, and I am myself. There's no space for compromise in our night-shrouded world.

5.

Pavio shows at 7:05, just less than an hour until the streetlights go out. She still dresses in dark jeans and sweaters, a hold-out against the recent trend towards vibrant colors and reflective stripes. She wears glasses with thick, black frames. Clips her hair, exposing the sharp angles of her skull. Lillian doesn't charge her when Pavio orders a cup of faux-coffee, and Pavio stops to breathe in the hickory scent as though she actually savors it. She waits for Lillian to head into the kitchen before she bothers to speak.

"How much have you got?" she says, no preamble. Pavio has a very low tolerance for bullshit.

"Five hundred mils," I tell her. "Give or a take. I haven't measured yet."

Pavio nods and sips. "I need eight minutes' worth. No payment up front. No questions asked."

I don't ask questions, because I don't want to know. When Pavio explains her projects to me, her intent disappears behind the melange of terminology. She's smarter than me. Well-read. Spent years at the local university, accumulating degrees and building interests. Expects other people to keep up with her brain, gets disappointed when we fail.

I do not want to disappoint her. We both know I will hand over the product, nearly two-thirds of my flask. Had it been anyone else, I would have laughed at the suggestion. Mentioned the rising prices as the auctions picked up speed. Shown them the messages on my phone offering sixty bucks a millimeter.

For Pavio, I close my eyes and try to do the math. Calculate the profit remaining once it supplies my sister, how much I'll regret the excess of the last few hours. I agree, as we both assume I will.

Pavio gives me a time and location. She finishes her drink and leaves.

Lillian re-emerges and shakes her head. "You shouldn't encourage her," she says. "You know how it will go down, yeah?"

I do, but I admit nothing. It's safer for us both.

"She's going to get in trouble," Lillian says. "They're watching out for people trying things outside the military labs."

I check my watch. "Twelve minutes to eight. Almost time for lights out."

Lillian frowns. I've hurt her feelings. "Mika," she says. "Come on, man. I—"

"Catch you tomorrow, yeah?"

I bail on our nascent argument, for all the good that does. We are all in trouble, now, every single one of us. We accept the endless darkness as normal, adapt as best we can, forget it could be any other way.

We accept, and in accepting, give in and subsist.

Pavio, at least, still believes in doing something. I respect that, as much as I'm able, while eking out a living.

6.

At Midnight, I check my phone. Run through the final bids. The contents of the flask will sell, on average, for one hundred and thirteen dollars a millimeter, portioned out between nine different buyers, a few seconds of daylight here. A whole minute to someone there.

Enough to keep me solvent, though it could have done far more.

7.

Wednesday morning. Eleven o'clock. The location Pavio gave me is three hundred kilometers down the coast, away from the streetlights that demark day and night. Stars fill the sky like the coarse grains on a sandpaper, as if the light is still out there beyond the darkness, trying to scour its way through.

Pavio has built a machine, a complex tangle of tubes and wiring connected to a generator. She's towed it out to this beach on a trailer, covered with a blue tarpaulin. When I show up, the warm bottle of daylight tucked into my satchel, hidden beneath dirty laundry in case I am stopped and searched, she is kneeling with a laptop perched on the towbar. Her computer connected to her apparatus, the screen bright in the darkness. I park my car and kill the engine, wait for the hula girl on my dash to go still. She seems less amusing now, here on a darkened beachside. Far from home, but so close to the ink-dark sea and the pale expanse of sand.

There's no pause in Pavio's work. No glance up to confirm it's me whose arrived. Pavio stays focused and waves me over with one hand, the other dancing across the keyboard. I slip her daylight from my bag.

"I'm still setting up," she says. "Diagnostic check."

I approach, studying her device with caution. Her projects are usually small, discrete. The size of a breadbox, or a chest of drawers, when she feels ambitious. Her machine is larger than my car, twice as tall as I am. Where did she source the materials? Where did she find the space?

"Trip down was bumpier than expected," she says. "Don't want to screw the first test up because a part rattled loose."

There are chimneys, six of them, the chassis built around their upright metal flues like the swollen roots of a tree. When I ask Pavio what needs doing, she points to the cap atop a bulbous tank. "Pour," she says. "Gently. Try not to spill it."

The bottle warms my chest and my steps are unsteady on the sand. I tip the daylight into the engine, thick as golden syrup. Daylight doesn't have a smell, but as it hits, the air long-forgotten scents unfurl: the heating steel of Pavio's machine; the smell of sun-warmed sand rising up, courtesy of the momentary exposure as the light funnels into the tank. Old memories resurrected by the moment of distilled warmth.

When I'm done, the bottle empty and cold, Pavio nods in satisfaction.

"All right," she said. "We're ready to go."

She produces a mask, thick steel with a black lens. The protection welders use, sitting close to the bright, molten solder. Pavio unearths a second, hands it to me.

"You might want to sit," she says.

8.

I have seen sixteen machines in operation before my sister's latest creation. They were frequently small devices, prototypes, reactors, and generators constructed to test a particular theory. This machine is no prototype. It is, perhaps, a culmination. As I slump to the sand it rumbles, metal ticking as it expands, responding to the warmth of the daylight running through its systems. It builds to a calamitous racket, like an engine pushed too hard, too fast. I tense, prepare to scramble, get the hell away before it blows, but Pavio touches my arm and holds me in place. She speaks, I think, behind her mask, but I do not hear it over the noise.

What emerges from those open flues is not the daylight of my youth, familiar and warm and unthinkingly *there* in a way we never noticed. What emerges is a torrent, six exploding geysers, expelled with sufficient force to lance the sky itself. A flare so bright I look away, one arm thrown against the tinted lens of my mask, spots dancing in front of my eyes. The rush of it sends grains of sand flying, stinging the exposed flesh on my hands, my neck, my ears.

Through the haze I can see it: the beach as it used to be. Lit up. Warm. Inviting. Hot dunes and blue waves and white shells and driftwood. The warmth that seeks a way in through your very pores, leaving your skin humming with the pleasure of being out there. I'm risking sunburn, actual sunburn, for the first time in years.

I do not hear the gunshots over the din of the machine. Do not know they have destroyed it until the light dims and the uniforms appear, swarming the beach with determined precision. The darkness reasserts itself, swarms in to fill the emptiness left behind as the sunlight fades.

There are sirens. There are guns. We are, quite thoroughly, busted. They cuff Pavio and take her away. This may, or may not, be an act of kindness. She's not forced to watch as three soldiers with machine guns annihilate her beloved, painstaking creation and ensure its destruction.

9.

They do not arrest me, though it's made clear that arrest is an option they're choosing not to pursue. The detectives who question me take the time to establish their benevolence. They will not arrest me, so long as I cooperate. So long as I answer questions, tell them what my sister's machine is meant to do and why I was there on the beach. I give them the truth, so far as I understand it, because I know so very little. I expect my lack of knowledge to anger them, but they release me after several hours and warn me to keep my nose clean.

They are still holding Pavio. Interrogations, they tell me. Further inquiries needed. When Katie ships me a flask of daylight, it's intercepted at the border. Her next attempt, and her last, sees her details given to the authorities and time spent in a Pennsylvania jail.

They will not let me see Pavio anymore. They authorities have laid no charges.

"She is doing necessary work," the officer managing Pavio's case informs me. "And she's cooperating. She's a smart cookie, best thing she could do right now."

"Cooperating with what?" I ask.

"Our investigation," the officer says, as if that answers anything.

10.

Days turn into weeks. They do not charge her, nor release her. They do not let me speak to her, nor let her make a phone call.

We gave up these civilized rules, once the darkness fell over the city. Regarded it as necessary, given how poorly we saw things amid the inky shadows of constant night.

In desperation, I ask for Lilian's help. "Talk to your uncle," I beg her. "Get me something."

"I'll see what I can do," she says, and shortly I receive a letter with Pavio's name at the end.

It arrives in my PO Box, the envelope taped shut after the military reviewed it, going through the contents to censor what is necessary with a kind of ruthless efficiently. Whole paragraphs expunged, wiped out by impenetrable black ink. Those that remain are banal, emotionless.

They promise she is okay, that her capture may be a good thing.

11.

Weeks later, I head to Lillian's café again. She's killing time, wiping the tables down now the dinner rush is over. Asks me if there's any news, as I settle in to peruse her menu.

"Pavio wrote me a letter," I tell her. "Heavily censored, from the looks of it, but she might be doing okay."

"A girl that smart..." Lillian says, and stops herself. She's been saying it a lot, as a source of comfort, ever since I asked for her help. A girl that smart, like Pavio, you don't want to see her talents go to waste. A girl that smart, like Pavio, you find a productive use for her capabilities. Lillian uses those four words so often, I wonder if they're truly hers, or something repeated after talking to her uncle.

She scrambles tofu and places it before me. "A girl that smart," I tell her, "deserves more than a world like this delivers."

"Pity she's stuck with this one, yeah?"

"Yeah," I say. "A pity."

At night the question plagues me: a girl that smart, like Pavio, you ever wonder what she was trying to do, with that big ol' machine? It prompts uncomfortable follow-up queries: What set the authorities on their trail? What, exactly, started the authorities searching, timed their arrival just in time to see Pavio's work up and running? A girl that smart, like Pavio, sixteen machines into her process and experienced in avoiding detection. Who did she trust that betrayed her to the authorities? What mistake drew their attention, at her moment of triumph?

I don't want to contemplate what this could imply, given the limited number of friendships my sister maintained on a day-to-day basis.

There is only one name that makes sense, but I don't want to admit the possibility.

12.

I take other jobs to keep my ends meeting. I drive a cab, then walk dogs, then end up working on the line of the local grocery. Scanning, bagging, taking payment. Cheerfully saying hello and goodbye, every time a customer comes through my station. Personal interaction is a competitive edge these days, a reprieve from the isolation engendered by too much darkness.

It isn't that I hate the job. One finds work where one can and musters the gratitude one can. I keep applying to the authorities for news of my sister, receive identical responses in return. Pavio's being held. Pavio's being questioned. She's helping with their enquiries, further details will be provided.

For weeks, I avoid Lillian's café. I cannot bring myself to face her, cannot leverage the doubts from my head and pretend it is like it was. When I break, uncertain, angry at myself, she seems very pleased to see me. She points to a chair at the counter, brews me fresh coffee and readies a plate of scramble. Waits for the room to clear before she comes over and makes small talk.

In the end, just before lights out, she says, "You gotta stop pushing for answers."

I blink at her, surprised.

"They're not going to let her go," she says. "They need her. She's too smart to be working rogue, dealing with the problem solo. They want her supervised, controlled. Resourced and networked with others like her, trying to find a solution."

For a second, I have no voice for questions. Lillian stands behind her counter, rubbing her hands with a coffee-stained rag. She lets me recover, process the news. "You asked again?"

"I asked," she says.

"And you believe your uncle? She's really okay?"

"Sometimes you've got to trust," she says. "If you push, they'll have to stop you. Send in a squad to make you disappear."

I am not okay with that idea. I do not want to disappear. But I do not want to drop it, stop pushing without confirmation that my sister's safe and happy.

"You knew it wouldn't last. Eventually, they'd catch up with her." Lillian reaches across the counter, puts her hand on top of mine. Her touch is soft and warm, gritty where the coffee-ground clings to her skin. "She's okay. I swear it. She's content."

It's so tempting to believe, to let the worry go. I look into Lillian's marvelous eyes, gray and bright and happy to see me. It occurs to me, not for the first time, that I no longer deal in daylight. I have an honest job and I earn honest money, and the old impediments that held us to friendship have ceased to be meaningful. All that remains to keep us apart are suspicions.

Then Lillian says: "Tell me about the light, when Pavio got that machine up and running. How'd it feel to see blue sky again? To see daylight in the sky?"

I look away and take a deep breath, ashamed of my own thoughts. Part of me still wants to hurt her, but the truth sticks in my throat.

"It wasn't blue," I tell her. "Not really. Not ever. Pavio explained it once, all wavelengths and angles. The blue comes from colors scattering differently when you shine up instead of on."

Then I pull my hand from hers, the warmth of her touch still lingering. I sit back and meet Lilian's stare, rub my palm against my jeans as I wonder how far to trust her.

"I could use another coffee," I say. "Before you're done for the night."

"I can only swing you a single freebie," she says. "The next one gets paid in cash."

I do not have that kind of money, but I order the coffee, anyway.

THE MIKE & CARLY STORY, WITHOUT THE GOSSIP

So the trouble starts with this: Mike likes Carly and Carly doesn't like him back. Mike's trying to figure the situation out as best he can, then he turns fifteen and this werewolf thing happens—boom—and he spends three nights a month camping out in the middle of nowhere because a pining teenage werewolf and the full moon aren't a great combination. It's enough to make you feel bad for the guy.

None of this is news, yeah? I mean, the werewolf thing, sure, but the rest is obvious. You catch the two of them together all the time, Carly with her wire-frame glasses and her hot-pink bob, Mike with his eyeliner and his older brother's black Nirvana shirt, and it's clear to everyone Mike never considered wearing mascara prior to Carly deciding she was into punk—*punk*, not *emo*—and Mike became punk-not-emo too, for real, trailing along after Carly, a private entourage of one.

No one missed Mike's crush, not even Carly. She's not stupid about these things, but she pretends she is so she doesn't have to hurt Mike's feelings. I mean, she likes Mike well enough; he's a nice guy, and he learned how to use eyeliner for her, and that's worth something in Carly's book. Problem is, she doesn't like Mike the way Mike likes her. She likes his older brother, Jake, that way. Possibly even someone like that loser Oscar Delluna. But Mike? No. A world of no. Never going to happen, and anyone who says otherwise has binged on too many romantic comedies.

Mike doesn't get that. Never really did. He figures Carly would like him if she could, but liking a werewolf is a tricky thing and invites nothing but hassle. Werewolves don't draw a line between love and hate and irritation, so it gets messy right about the point where they grow fur. The fact that Carly might not like him, Mike-Mike rather than Werewolf-Mike, hasn't even crossed Mike's mind. He's good with computers, Mike, and he's stubborn like you wouldn't believe. He really is a werewolf, too. Limited group of folks in the loop about that. I figure you deserve to know, since I'm trying to tell you the whole story, the Carly-and-Mike story. Some of it's meant to be a secret, but it's just between us—and Mike's a lot cooler with the werewolf thing these days. If you keep quiet about Carly kinda-sorta liking Oscar Delluna and everything'll be fine. 'Course Oscar Delluna's a creep, so you probably shouldn't talk to him anyway, not unless you're working to figure out exactly what Carly saw in him. Me, I've never truly understood.

Anyway, Mike's a werewolf and it involves a lot of camping. Mike isn't big on the camping, even though his parents insist it's the only way. His parents are werewolves too, so they know what they're talking about. Mike-Mike hates the great outdoors, although by all accounts Werewolf-Mike's ecstatic as heck once the moon is in the sky. He gets to run and howl and roll in the dust. He hunts down kangaroos and gets into fights with the wild pigs. Sometimes Mike wakes up the morning after and he's in the middle of nowhere—even more in the middle of nowhere than he was at the start of the camping trip—and it takes him hours to hike barefoot through the bush and find his parents again.

He spends most of those walks speculating about Carly, wondering what she's been doing for the last couple of days. Mike predicts worst-case scenarios. Carly kissed Jake at a party, or she talked to Oscar Delluna when he came into the video store where Carly works, or Carly knows that Werewolf-Mike isn't one for the eyeliner and that's what's costing Mike-Mike his shot. Those kinds of thoughts drive Mike nuts, month after month, right up until the morning he comes back from camping and finds out that Carly really has kissed Oscar Delluna at a party.

It wasn't a good kiss, by all accounts. It turns out Oscar Delluna made out with Carly on a dare, proving to his buddies he could, and no one was particularly satisfied by the experience, least of all Carly. Mike doesn't know this right away, but they're coming back from the camping trip the day after it all went down and there Carly is, waiting on the front steps, wanting to tell Mike what happened because she figures Werewolf-Mike can get mean and wolf-like to defend her honor. Mike gets out of his parents' Range Rover and shoulders his pack. He walks up to Carly and says, "Hi."

Carly looks up and smiles, but it's a weak little smile rather than the wicked grin Mike loves, and he realizes instantly that big things happened while he was away.

"Hi," Carly says. "How was the trip?"

Mike shrugged. He's covered in dirt and he ripped his second-favorite T-shirt when he turned into a wolf. Right now Mike's wishing he'd thought to take his eyeliner pen out camping with him. Carly looks down at her shoes and taps her toes together, wishing there was some way she could ask Mike to hurt Oscar Delluna without telling him what happened. Mike's parents, who know an awkward pause when they see one, choose this exact moment to bustle past and carry the gear into the house. Not that Mike's family takes a lot of gear with them when they go camping. Going wolf cuts down on their need for a tent.

"Listen," Carly says, "I've need a favor. A big one. The kind where I ask you to do something and you don't ask why."

She's still looking at her shoes, wondering when her right toenail punched a hole in her favorite pair of pink Converse, and Mike sits down next to her and nudges her with his elbow. Carly's got nail polish on her feet, candy-apple red, and you can see the polish on her big toe through the crack in her sneakers.

"No questions asked?" Mike says. "That's some favor." But here's the tragedy of the moment—Mike doesn't need to ask questions. Not around that time of the month. He's still got a little bit of the wolf in him after a night in the bush and that means he can scent the harsh cigarette smoke on Carly's lips, a brackish-sweet mix of tobacco and cloves. Mike knows that Carly doesn't smoke. Hell, there's only one guy at school who smokes that brand of cigarettes, and Mike's smart enough to put two and two together.

That's one of the problems with being a werewolf that nobody thinks to tell you about. Everyone focuses on the big problems—hurting the people you love, accidentally killing some farmer's sheep, getting shot by overzealous monster hunters who assume you're a menace because you change shape three nights a month—but nobody considers the little problems, the impracticalities of living with a wolf's nose and a wolf's ears. No one thinks about the way you now figure things out that you'd rather stay ignorant about, not unless they suddenly find themselves in a position like Mike's and wishing they weren't. You'd think there's an upside to the whole werewolf thing to make up for the inconvenience, but mostly it's an enormous hassle.

"No questions asked," Mike says. He grits his teeth and forces down the lump in his throat. He balls his fists into tight knots and wishes he could hit something. He keeps his voice calm. "Sure, I can do that, I guess."

Carly, she doesn't notice any of this. She's not a werewolf, so she smells things and hears things like the rest of us, and mostly she's watching her shoes like they're opening up a broadway show. Carly's embarrassed by what happened and wishing she hadn't kissed Oscar Delluna last night. She's also wishing she could try kissing him again, just in case, because there's a possibility he really liked her and used the dare to kiss her without giving his true feels away. And Werewolf-Mike could really hurt Oscar, maybe even kill him. Mike's parents always said that Mike has no understanding of what he's doing when he's all wolfed up, running on instinct, and it could be her plan is majorly bad idea. So Carly sits next to Mike, bouncing her feet, doubting whether she should really ask him what she was going to ask him, and then she says, "Never mind. Sorry, no big deal, just wondering if you'd do it, you know? Just testing."

Mike nods and gives Carly an encouraging smile. "I'd do it," he says. "Anything you ask, you know that." He yawns and stretches, spine popping as he arcs his back. Carly smiles at him, all sad and cute, and it's one of those moments when Mike knows how much he likes her real deep in his gut.

"Come around later," she says. "I got a bunch of old horror flicks from work."

Carly likes horror movies. Mike doesn't, but he pretends that he does, because it's an excuse to hang out with Carly.

"Sure," he says. "After dinner. Call me."

Then Carly walks off and Mike's left standing there, the scent of Oscar Delluna's cigarette smoke tickling his nose, wondering what really went on while he was camping. Mike's still got enough of the wolf riding shotgun that he's tempted to do something bad right then. He really, really wants to track Oscar Delluna down and bite him, hard, right where it'd hurt. Werewolf-Mike would go do it without hesitation, because Werewolf-Mike is an angry ball of sharp teeth and fur-covered muscle. Unfortunately, Mike-Mike is scrawny and half Oscar Delluna's size, so he bites down on the urge and goes inside instead. He lies on his bed, staring at the wall, the volume of his stereo turned up so loud that he can't think straight. That's good because thinking leads to knowing stuff and knowing stuff leads to trouble.

Mike's been in his room for an hour or two before his brother knocks on the door, hammering it with a big fist, then barges in without bothering to wait for permission. Mike's brother Jake is a big guy, good looking. He even got away with being an ordinary guy, despite his parents—there's no full moon camping trips for him, not even when he was a kid. It happens sometimes, when both the parents are werewolves. Jake got lucky, Mike inherited the genetics.

"Hey, fuzzball," Jake says. "What's up?"

Mike mumbles an answer that might be nothing and might be varmint, but Jake can't be sure given the pillow over Mike's face. Jake sits on the bed and punches his brother in the leg.

"Let's try that again, fuzzy. What's up?"

This time Mike snaps the pillow away and sits up, glaring at Jake.

"Nothing," Mike says. "Nothing, okay?"

Mike's been crying. You can tell because no one taught Mike about not applying eyeliner before you leak tears. He has black streaks down his face, like someone has been oiling up his eyeballs. Jake backs off, hands in the air. He settles down on the far end of the bed, watching his little brother crumple back against the bed-head. Jake has his flaws—he's oblivious to the fact that Carly likes him, for starters—but he's basically okay and he cares about Mike more than Jake lets on. Wolves are pack animals, so they try to get along. Jake isn't a werewolf, but werewolves raised him. The habit kind of sticks. "Seriously, Mike," Jake says. "What's up?"

"Carly," Mike says. "She kissed someone else at a party and aftermath wasn't good. I could smell it."

"Ah," Jake says. He's got a fair idea of what happened. He was at that party, after all, and you pick up the gossip. Everyone did, even you, which is why I'm here, setting the record straight. Jake might be oblivious to Carly liking him, but he's smart enough to know how Mike feels about her. Jake's also got a fair idea of what Mike's contemplating at that very moment, and there're decent odds that Jake's fair idea is dead accurate.

Jake says, "You want to talk about it?"

So Mike tells Jake what's happened, about the cigarettes lingering on Carly's lips and the thing she didn't ask Mike to do, and Jake listens and nods and asks questions in all the right places. Then Jake says, "I was at that party, you know," and Mike says, "Oh," and Jake says, "Yeah."

"If it were me," Jake says, "and if I was obsessing this way, and if I was a werewolf, then I'd go do something about it right away. Right now. Because even if it didn't work, you'd have done *a thing* and if you don't do something while you're you…"

Jake lets that thought trail off, but Mike knows which direction to go and he nods. Jake's thinking about the next full moon, about Werewolf-Mike and that tendency that a werewolf who's angry with a guy, the kind of angry that boils deep down in your bone marrow… well, it's not pretty. You tend to worry for that bloke the werewolf is mad at when the next full moon arrives. Mike's been a pretty good werewolf. He hasn't really hurt anyone since all this started, except for the wild pigs, and it seems like the pigs always start those fights. So Mike and Jake sit there for a while, pondering this, and eventually Jake pats his brother on the shoulder, all awkward and not really comforting, and goes downstairs to watch TV.

And Mike does do something, the only thing he can imagine doing for his best friend. Mike goes next door and watches horror movies with Carly, closing his eyes in the scary bits, pretending he doesn't notice how she smells like plasticky-lipstick and someone else's cigarette smoke. Pretending he doesn't recognize the sick churn in his stomach, the one that's kind of like that warm, angry feeling he gets after eating too much porridge.

Later, after they're tired of watching feral clowns disemboweling American college kids with steel hooks and chainsaws, Mike and Carly sit on the couch in Carly's lounge room, not doing anything really, idle channel surfing. And after they've done that for a while, long enough to figure out that there's nothing on, Mike takes a deep breath and says, "So I know you kissed Oscar Delluna," only he says it real soft, like he hopes that Carly won't actually catch him saying it, and he doesn't take his eyes off the dancing gummy bear that fills the TV screen. Except Carly does hear him, loud and clear, and she puts the TV remote down on the arm of her parents' paisley green couch and says, "Oh."

"Did Jake tell you?" Carly asks, because she remembers that Jake was there and she was really hoping Jake hadn't heard, given he's nicer than Oscar Delluna and generally more interesting, even though Jake has never really noticed Carly as anything more than Mike's friend from next door. Mike nods, a white lie, because he'd prefer not to discuss being a werewolf, not right now, and Jake probably would have told him, sooner or later, maybe.

"You wanted me to bite him," Mike adds. "Before, when you came over, that's what you were going to ask."

"Yeah," Carly says. "I guess."

"I will, you know," Mike says. "If you still want me too."

"No," Carly says. "It's okay."

And then Carly tells Mike the whole story, even though Mike doesn't really wish to hear it, because Carly needs a friend and Mike's always been there and he's a good listener despite all his other faults. She tells Mike about Oscar's sloppy kisses came with an aftertaste like ashes and the way Oscar Delluna disappeared when she ducked off to the bathroom. About catty Caitlyn Morse, who bailed up Carly while she was searching the party for Oscar, and how Caitlin explained Oscar had been dared to make out with Carly by Glen Dougherty and how Glen owed Oscar twenty bucks for going through with it. And about that itty bitty part of Carly that still wishes that Oscar Delluna would kiss her again. Launch into an elaborate, detailed explanation about hiding his true feelings behind the bet. Because, if you like someone enough, it's scary. And you really want to forgive them for being a gosh darn idiot.

"He won't, you know," Mike says. "It doesn't work that way, liking someone. It sucks, but it doesn't."

And he knows right then that Carly is about to cry, because he can smell the tears coming before Carly even knows she's about to cry them. It's the least punk-rock thing Mike has ever seen Carly do.

"I think I will bite him," Mike says. "Stupid Oscar Delluna. I'll chomp his ass so hard."

"Don't," Carly says. "You'll hurt him, really bad. Isn't that what your parents say?"

"I'm not waiting for the full moon," Mike says. "Tomorrow. It's going down tomorrow. I'm going to bite him at school."

And right then Carly looks over at Mike, and she sees a flash of Werewolf-Mike, right there, in Mike-Mike's eyes. A quick glimpse, like seeing a goldfish at the bottom of the pond, then it's gone. The only one left is Mike-Mike, and he runs out of the room, heading home because he's so angry that he's going to cry and he really doesn't want to do that in front of Carly. Carly watches him go, holding her breath.

I don't really need to tell you what happens next.

I mean, everyone knows this part. Mike jumps Oscar Delluna at school, just runs up and leaps on him while Oscar's eating lunch with Glen Dougherty and Barry Wilde and that real mean kid that everyone calls Panzo. Everyone was there for the fight, even if it wasn't much of a fight. A few seconds of Mike trying to gnaw Oscar's ear off before Barry and Glen and Panzo got involved. After that Mike was on the ground, getting kicked to hell and bleeding all over the concrete. No one wins a fight once Panzo gets involved, so Mike was doomed from the start, even if it wasn't four on one.

Eventually, Mr. Cook broke things up and Mike scored a suspension, because everyone confirmed he'd started it, even though most folks assumed Oscar Delluna deserved to get bitten. It seemed unfair, especially with Oscar Delluna bragging about it, but two days later Jake found Oscar alone on the bike-track behind Coles and got a little bit of revenge for his brother. I guess Oscar Delluna was kinda cute once upon a time, even if he's never been nice, but you just don't look cute once someone's broken your nose.

Mike's parents weren't happy about the suspension, but they did their best to understand—they'd both been teenage werewolves themselves, once upon a time, so they get how hard it gets. They grounded Mike, which meant he spent most of his suspension holed up in his room going all emo—*emo*, not *punk*—over the fact that Carly stopped talking to him.

And somewhere between then and now the gossip started, and you'd start hearing things, like Mike and Carly were actually going out and Carly cheated on Mike with Oscar, and that's why he went insane. Or you'd be told that Carly was going out with Jake, and that she'd cheated on Jake with Mike, and that Oscar was just trying to do the right thing by proving she was doing the dirty on the side. I even heard that Mike really bit off Oscar Delluna's ear in the fight, and that right now Oscar Delluna's got a pig's ear instead, that you can see the scars if you fold the top of his ear down and look real close.

None of that stuff's true, it's gossip. And now I've told you the real story, the Carly-and-Mike story, the way I know it. Mike and Carly still aren't talking, and Mike's still emo for her, and Carly isn't exactly happy about all this either. She misses Mike, just a little, not the way he'd like her to miss him, but as a friend. They haven't talked for twenty-six days now, not since that night after the last full moon, and tomorrow night's the full moon and Mike's mum has been on the phone with all his friends, struggling to track him down. Mike wasn't at school yesterday, or the day before, and his family hasn't seen him since he said he was going for a ride on Thursday afternoon. They're meant to go camping tomorrow night. They're trying to plan for what happens next if Mike doesn't come home.

Me, I saw Mike yesterday, riding his bike along the path on Timothy Road that leads into the national park. I tried to say hello, but he breezed on by without saying anything. Near as I can tell, that was the last anyone's seen him. Mike's parents think he's hiding out in the park, waiting for the moonrise. They're worried. So is Carly. And if Oscar Delluna understood half of what I've told you today, you can bet that he'd be pissing his pants thinking about the next full moon too. Because there's eight hours of moonlight and Werewolf-Mike's nose picks up way more than Mike-Mike's nose can, and no one's sure what will happen when Werewolf-Mike shows up. Not you, not me, not Mike-Mike or Werewolf-Mike or poor Carly in the middle of things.

All we can do is watch the moonrise and wait.

A WHITE CROSS BESIDE A LONELY ROAD

ONE

Alex and Brendan live in the decrepit house on Norfolk Road, the place with a leaking corrugated iron roof and water-stains on the bedroom wall, the constant dripping through the long, wet summers leaving the carpet patched with a strange, white mold. The house where the scents of the Brisbane River blow through in the afternoon, slipping past gaps at the floor where skirting boards should be. The house where Alex can see his breath plume as he exhales every winter, the June cold seeping through the layers of cloth and wool he uses to ward it off. It's a miserable house when the cold hits, but it mirrors Alex's mood far more often than not. Matches his urge to lash out at Brendan, his frustration with their choices.

Right now the evening air is thin and sharp, offers too little resistance to the cutting barbs as they talk about the trip. "Our words slip out too easily, this time of the year," Brendan says. "There's not enough humidity to blunt the stupid shit going on in our heads."

He's trying to make the best of it. Blunt force attempts to make Alex laugh and think of better times. Desperate to keep the fight they're having now from escalating into the fight they don't want to have. The one where Alex says the words he can't take back.

Every month is miserable in that house, but at least winter is dry. The summer storms and the rotten carpet always make it feel so much worse. Alex acknowledges he should get onto that, do more than set up buckets and towels to catch the condensation that rolls down the walls. He recognizes he should replace the carpet, clean the place so it no longer smells of mildew and old Thai curry and whatever candles or incense Brendan's been burning to cover up the stink.

Alex acknowledges he should be on top of these things, but instead he's packing a duffle bag. Folding jumpers and feeding them into the floppy maw, then wondering if they'll be warm enough. His toes are already numb inside his Docs, and it will be colder as he heads west.

Brendan is out on the balcony, smoking cigarettes and brooding. They've been arguing, again. Or arguing, still. Alex is no longer certain when the arguments start and when they stop. The cigarette smoke drifts in through the open window, followed by the hoppy scent of the brewery across the river.

Alex shifts his attention to the pile of rumpled, threadbare t-shirts. Folds them, one-by-one, and place them on top of his jumpers. Does his underwear. Socks. Searches the clean laundry for his handkerchiefs. When he turns around, Brendan is there, loitering at the bedroom door. Brendan, skinny and pale and fey. Dark hair, long lashes, black-painted fingernails French-tipped with tiny half-moons of silver. Brendan picks at the ancient paint-job on the doorjamb, peeling flakes in thin, fragile strips.

"Hey," he says, and Alex doesn't answer. Doesn't want to be the person who kicks off this next round of bickering. Doesn't want to be the one who finds a permeation they've not yet argued to death.

Alex gathers up his handkerchiefs. He tells himself he's busy now, too busy to talk.

· · ·

Brendan clears his threat, a bid for attention. Alex feeds hanky pile into the bag, wonders whether six will be enough for a weekend. It's a cheap ploy, withdrawing, but it's what he's got right now.

It doesn't stop Brendan from holding forth. "Thirty-two candles on your birthday cake this year," he says. "Consider that, yeah?"

Alex stops packing and sits down beside the duffle, his shoulders sagging beneath the weight of the conversation loitering in the wings. "You didn't make me a cake," he says.

"Wouldn't have bothered with candles, either. That's not the point."

"Illuminate me," Alex says. "What *is* the point you're making?"

"I'm saying you are thirty-two. You got your own house, a job, a guy to love. It's probably time to stop fearing what your parents think, yeah?"

"Yeah, fuck you," Alex says.

This is the truth as Brendan sees it. As if there's no other reason for Alex to head back to Charleville alone, pretending his boyfriend doesn't exist. Everything comes down to Alex's fear, and it's not like Brendan's wrong.

There's just no speculation about the source of Alex's fear. Brendan assumes, and in doing so, neglects any other cause.

Alex sinks into the bed, closes his eyes, and lets his head fall into the soft caress of blankets. He rubs his face with both hands, trying to scrub away the familiar exhaustion of the fight. "I'm not afraid of my parents," he says. "Things are more complicated than that."

The mattress tilts as Brendan settles beside him. A blackened fingernail runs down Alex's leg. "You always say that, 'Lex."

"That's because it's invariably true." Alex takes one of Brendan's hands, holds it as sucks a deep breath and forces himself to stay calm. "My reluctance isn't about you, not the way you think. I didn't particularly enjoy growing up back home."

"Who does?"

Alex pauses and furrows his brow, searching for some sign of understanding in Brendan's kohl-rimmed eyes. He doesn't see it. He doesn't expect too. That's how these arguments go. Brendan is a Brisbane guy. Grew up on the south side. A quiet, suburban house and two parents who stayed together until the cancer did his mother in and his father faded away. Brendan is only twenty-three, young enough that the internet was there right from his earliest days. Brendan quits jobs because they bore him, moves on to another interest. Or waits, biding his time for a while, content to pick up unemployment while hunting for the next gig. His existence defined by access: to the city; to the world; to people just like him.

Alex remembers the time before the house on Norfolk Road. Still reacts like a country boy after fourteen years there. Still gets surprised when he can leave his house and get a latte on a Sunday morning. He's given up trying to explain that disconnection to Brendan. "I know about pain," the younger man says. "I know about feeling alone, 'Lex."

No, Alex thinks. *You really don't.*

But there's no route to clarifying the difference without making things so much worse.

Brendan places a kiss on Alex's shoulder, just above the collarbone. The soft prickle of afternoon stubble grazing the skin as he moves along. "Twenty-four candles on my birthday cake this year," he says. "Maybe not as many as you, but I'm a big boy. I was taking care of myself before we met."

"It won't be fun," Alex says.

"But you'll be there."

The tone's so sweet, so serious, that Alex wants to burst out laughing. Then there's the gentle nudge of Brendan's nose, the long kisses that work their way across Alex's collar; the first phase of the distraction that ends the argument and all attempts to pack.

TWO

The next night, heading out past Gatton. The ancient Holden gobbling down highway, making good time along the bitumen vein slicing through the fields of tobacco and dormant sunflowers waiting for sunrise. Two hours into the ten-hour trek, Alex keeping his eyes on the horizon, the dark silhouettes of the foothills and the mountains beyond. His fingers wrapped around the broken indicator arm to keep the high beams active and pointed at the road. A distraction to prevent himself from cataloging all the problems with his car.

And Brendan? Brendan's bored, just like Alex expected him to be. Hunting for new songs on the tape deck. No longer attempting to start conversations, not after the way Alex snapped at him while they were going through Ipswich.

The broken speedometer says they're doing sixty Ks an hour, but experience says they're really going twice as fast. Brendan finds the song he's looking for and lets it play, crooning along with Nico in a cracked falsetto as the opening verse of *Pale Blue Eyes* distorts in the ancient speakers. Lou Reed's guitar is fuzzy, the lyrics half-lost in the auditory bleed.

Alex grits his teeth. There problems with the cassette deck sticks in his gut; he's over thirty now, working a good job. He should be able to afford a better car than the Holden, one that runs on more than stubborn faith and gaffer tape. Alex is sure it's dangerous to push the ancient vehicle this hard, but he finds it difficult to care. He tries, he wants to force himself to feel something, but there's nothing left inside him. He's numbed to it all, waiting for life to change. Figures it for Brendan's turn to do the changing.

Brendan leans his head against the window, stares at the landscape. Alex catches sight of his reflection in the dirty windscreen: the narrow face; the dark eyeliner; the delicate steel ring in his nose.

The song ends. The tape deck hisses. Brendan says, "Do you think they'll like me?"

They. Alex's parents.

"Of course," Alex says. "They get on with everyone. My parents always do."

He tries to fend off the reasons that statement is a lie. Struggles not to list them, starting with Brendan's age. With his black hair and eye-shadow and boots with shiny silver buckles. The violet lipstick. The lack of a regular job. The fact that Brendan's dating their son.

The possibilities continue to froth up, like the fizz that rushes from a freshly dropped can of coke.

Don't think about it. Drive. Keep your focus on the road.

They speed through Hatton Vale, heading for the Gap. Brendan says, "They know you date boys, right?"

He's grinning. Bad jokes to diffuse the tension, because that's what Brendan does.

"Yeah," Alex says. "They've known for a while."

But they haven't seen it up close.

Brendan swaps the tape out, The Velvet Underground giving way to *Appetite for Destruction*. Old tapes from Alex's childhood, preserved here in the ancient vehicle that will only play cassettes.

"Your taste was shit in high school," Brendan says.

Alex doesn't answer. He turns the stereo up; lets the speakers bleed the song into white noise. Brendan goes back to singing, his voice loud enough to insert lyrics where distortion makes the original singer incomprehensible.

They spend the first leg of the trip in their own heads, all the way into Toowoomba. Then a pit-stop at the twenty-four-hour Caltex on Ruthven Street. Not that they need a twenty-four-hour—it's only ten PM and even Toowoomba doesn't shut all the way down at that time of the night. And the Holden is three-quarters full, good enough to get them a lot further inland before filling up is mandatory.

But Brendan wants to pee and Alex needs a break from his presence, so they pull in and split up to fulfill their appointed tasks. Brendan heads for the kiosk to beg for a toilet key. Alex slots the nozzle into the Holden and watches the dollars and cents accumulate. Hopes to hell he can keep things under twenty bucks.

There are motels flanking the street on both sides. Three stories and big signs, empty lots for visitors to park.

Every sign advertises a vacancy for weary travelers who want to stay overnight.

The night they met, Brendan took hold of Alex's right hand and studied the palm intently. Alex recalls the surety of Brendan's touch, the tickle of a black thumbnail tracing the delicate groove of his love-line. He remembers the quiet pressure keeping his hand still while Brendan read.

"This indicates you should come with me," Brendan said, and Alex blinked in response.

"What?"

"You want me," Brendan said. "And the two of us belong together."

"You can see that in my palm?"

Brendan grinned, a gothic Cheshire Cat with pale cheekbones and ink-dark, spiked hair.

"It's there too," he said, and kept a tight grip on Alex's fingers. Brendan refused to let go until the party ended.

Brendan is out of the bathroom when Alex heads in to pay. The woman staffing the counter is pushing fifty. She's small, red curls, black-framed spectacles, Mobil polo shirt in navy blue with a nametag on her chest. The tag identifies her as Maureen, block capitals printed and taped over another name. Maureen surveys her kingdom of bowsers, foil-wrapped chocolate, refrigerators full of drinks, barely seems to notice the world beyond.

Brendan is selecting a strawberry milk from the refrigerator as Alex walks in. Maureen keeps Brendan under observation, not bothering to hide her suspicion. Alex stops at the doorway, doors sliding shut behind him. It's warm in the heated kiosk, among the candy bars and magazines. Alex watches Maureen watching Brendan, and wonders if he truly blames her.

It's not like Brendan hasn't engaged in petty theft. Alex has seen the spoils of his work over the last two years: pilfered lighters, confectionary, erasers, and pencils from the local supermarket. Once, a set of charcoal sticks from the art supply store in Lutwyche, the precursor to a six-month stint where Brendan dedicated himself to producing dark, abstract illustrations Alex never truly understood.

They no longer go to bookstores together. Not since the visit to Bent Books, near the city, when Brendan walked out with a paperback of real-life ghost stories tucked beneath his jacket.

Alex pays for the fuel, two Mars Bars, a can of coke, and Brendan's milk. It empties his account for the rest of the trip, no way home until he gets paid in two days. When they arrive, they're at his parent's mercy, but he's gotten used to that.

On the road again, leaving the city limits. Follow the highway west. Fret about the unsteady snarl of the Holden, Brendan flicking through the tapes. Alex skolling his can of coke, sucking down caffeine and sugar to keep him awake.

Brendan says, "How far is Longreach from your folks' place?"

"Five hours. Maybe six."

"Oh," Brendan says, and the silence that follows is pregnant with an unspoken desire.

"We're not going to Longreach," Alex says.

"I know." Brendan drums his fingers against his thigh. "It's just, you know, I was thinking…"

Alex knows what Brendan is expecting to happen: he wants to do the ghost tour through the Longreach Cemetery. Walk among the ancient headstones and the red dust. Twenty-five dollars a head, plus the fuel to haul arse all the way out there. Snacks for the road, something to drink. Navigate the highways, trusting the Holden to keep running. Get them there, get them back to his parent's place, get them back to Brisbane again.

"No," Alex says, and Brendan pouts. A sure sign there will be a second round before the fight's done, another attempt to get Alex onboard.

At least Alex knows why Brendan wanted to be part of the trip this time. Why he made so much noise about Alex never taking him out bush.

The rush of road, the white-ghost gum trees flicking in and out of the high beams. Brendan still singing along with the tape deck, the same off-key falsetto that Alex can only imagine coming from Brendan's lips. Occasional expanses of darkness, dairy paddocks, the shadows of sleeping cows against the limits of the car lights.

White crosses by the bitumen, memorials for those who died. Sparser, on rural highways, than they are in the city. Out here, on roads where pedestrians are rare, each cross is more likely to mark the death of somebody inside a vehicle. Victims of speeding, taking a corner fast. Or driving late and falling asleep at the wheel, hitting a tree or drifting across the dividing line and into the path of a road train.

Brendan slips a fresh cassette into the shitty stereo. Portishead. *Dummy*. Maudlin beats and tragic longing. He sings along with Beth Gibbons. His falsetto, clear and velvet-wrapped, a counterpoint to the fuzz of the speakers. Uninhibited and unconcerned, pantomiming the abject sadness inherent in the song.

And for a moment—a glorious flash—Alex remembers why they fell in love.

It's coming up on midnight, nearly halfway there. Alex misses the question the first time Brendan asks it. Undeterred, Brendan kills the sound. Clears his throat and leans forward, peering through the dusty windshield. "You ever get scared, out here at night?"

"No."

Brendan's curled on the front seat, heavy boots digging into battered upholstery. One hand still taps out a rhythm on the dash, the other supports his chin. He's watching the dark shadows slide by on the roadside, half-lit by the glow of the dashboard. Paler than normal, in the dim light.

"It's a lonely road," Brendan says.

"It's a highway."

"A lonely highway," he insists. "Anything could happen."

Alex makes the mistake of asking for examples. Brendan makes the mistake of explaining: urban legends about killers with hooks for hands, hitchhiking ghosts and escaped mental patients. The urban legends followed by weirder things, demented dreams from message boards and websites. *This meme I saw on Facebook that is plausible and real. This thing that happened on YouTube, I can send you the link when we have signal.*

"All of that seems unlikely," Alex says. "Unlikely, and far too American."

"But possible," Brendan says. "They *could* happen, right?"

"Not really."

"Not really isn't no," he says.

Alex bites down on a weary sigh. "No, but it's damn close."

THREE

At night, back home, sometimes Alex watches Brendan sleep. Wonders if it's really love, this thing that keeps them living together. The thing that keeps them talking, after all the stupid shit Brendan pulls. After all Alex does to keep them afloat, when Brendan walks away from another job, another passion, another career.

Five hours down. Cattle country. Paddocks fringed with barbed wire fences on both sides of the road. Prickly pear growing on the embankment. Air whistling through the open windows. Probably doing a hundred clicks an hour. Maybe a hundred and twenty.

Brendan says, "What happens if we crash?"

"We crash," Alex says. "Why?"

"Just thinking." Brendan shifts, turning forward, peering through the windshield. "There's nothing out here, you know?

Just farms and the occasional truck. Not like when shit goes wrong back home. If you wreck a car there, someone will notice. Help is on its way. Here—" he gestures at the empty highway "—who the fuck will find you before you bleed out?"

Five hours and twenty minutes down. More paddocks. More prickly pear. More Brendan.

"You ever pondered why Aussies don't urban myth shit the way Americans do," he said. "Dead Man's Curve. Suicide Drive. All those lonely, haunted roads where the legends get their start. We're a big country, same as they are. Plenty of open roads and isolated places where ghost stories could take root."

"We have ghost stories," Alex says.

"Not real ones."

"They're ghost stories. How real do you need?"

"I dunno. Just… vital. Plausible."

Alex says nothing, because that's easier. Because the other option is saying everything, and once that starts he isn't sure he'll stop. He picks his next words, examines each to ensure the nuance is right.

"I think you're being a snob."

"Yeah?"

"Yeah, city boy," Alex says, and he's tempted to smile. "Plenty of local legends build up, if you know a place. No different here than anywhere else."

Brendan scrunches his fingers, the little flutter of movement going still. "Convince me."

"No."

"Come on."

"*No.*"

"Dude, you totally want to," Brendan says. "Right now you're dying to prove me wrong, yeah?"

"I'm trying to drive here," Alex says, and he knows it's a mistake. He can hear the petulance creeping into his tone, phase one of an epic sulk that could infect the rest of the trip. Still, his eyes ache from staying focused on the road; his nerves scraped raw by nagging doubts. He can feel their relationship stretching, a taut line trailing all the way back to Brisbane and the argument in the house on Norfolk Road, tight and ready to snap if either of them makes a wrong step.

"Tell me a local legend," Brendan says. "Take me past a haunted stretch of highway, if they're so bloody common."

"Fuck off," Alex says.

"Because you can't do it."

"Because I'm tired. I want this over, and I'm not a fucking tourist."

The road through heading into Dalby gives Alex a moment of panic. Tight curves and dropping speed limits, trusting in the Holden's worn brake pads and Alex's control.

Brendan stares at the landscape, fascinated. Still clinging to his theories about ghosts and lonely roads. "So," he says, drawing the word out. "Have you, like, ever known somebody who died on the road?"

It's an innocent enough question, but Alex flinches, regardless. "Once," he says. "A friend of mine from high school careened into the trees with her boyfriend." He takes a deep breath, blinks a few times. "They reckon he was drunk."

"Were you the guy dating her?"

"No," Alex says.

"But you were friends?"

"Kind of."

"Shit. I'm sorry," Brendan says, and for once the sincerity is real.

Alex's knot of irritation doesn't leave his stomach, but it eases, gets enough slack they could unravel it. He cuts Brendan a break. "You didn't know," he says. "And I don't talk about it."

Neither of them speaks for the next hundred meters.

Then Brendan says, "You were taking those corners fast, yeah?"

There's a note of warning in his voice, a thread of concern that's normally absent. Usually, Alex is the sensible one. Usually, Alex's tasked with pulling Brendan back.

· · ·

It's not that Alex doesn't love Brendan, not really. He knows they've had plenty of good times. Conversations that aren't cold wars, arguments that get resolved and put away for good.

It's not that he doesn't love Brendan. It's just that he's not sure.

The Holden's growl gets deeper as it speeds up up an incline, a thin whine developing in the hollow's of the engine's snarl. The high beams drop with every curve, the broken arm falling back any time Alex needs two hands to control the wheel.

"You should get that fixed," Brendan says, watching the lights flicker as they round another corner.

Alex nods, grim, adding it to the list of problems that afflict the ancient vehicle. The Holden runs on stubborn hope and necessity; Alex cannot afford a new car, not now, not while they're both living on his salary.

"No big deal," he says, trying to convince himself. "Normally it's daylight when I'm swinging through here."

That's a lie as well.

FOUR

They make good time, drive through Morven a few minutes ahead of 4 AM. An hour away from Charleville, from the house with the twin water tanks and the mulberry tree in the backyard. Familiar roads leading back to his childhood home, and Alex thinks about arriving for breakfast. *Mum. Dad. This is Brendan.*

Another hundred Ks of driving, following the Warrego Highway.

He takes a right, heading north. The Landsborough threading towards Augathella. The artery that will take them to Longreach, to Isa. As far north as Alex can imagine going. Not the route they need, and even Brendan sees it, raising his head and blinking owlishly at the road sign filled with unfamiliar names and distances.

He pushes upright, shaking off the drowsiness. "Where we headed?"

"A detour," Alex says. "You wanted to see bits of home, yeah?"

He figures there's two hours until sunrise, at this time of the year. Alex keeps his fingers on the high beams, tries to remember the way. It's been years since he drove the backstreets, did anything other than follow the road to his parent's front door and hunkered down in the house for a few days. He's got no desire to see the old town, to catch up with friends who were glad when Alex moved away. He may not feel like a city boy, but he doesn't belong here either.

Alex takes a left turn off the main highway, bumps onto a red dirt track threading through the scrubby scrubland. A bush-bash trail between the Landsborough and the Mitchell, another half-hour or more to their journey even if everything goes right.

The Holden complains about the uneven terrain, engine whining as he speeds down the road. "That doesn't sound healthy," Brendan says.

"Not like we can fix it now," Alex says. "Maybe when you've found a new job, and we've got some extra cash."

"You sound like my mother," Brendan says. "And you're not her."

Alex braced to snap back, a brilliant retort on his lips. The start of an unraveling. Give a voice to the seeds of irritation that will grow into hatred, a separation, a decoupling of their lives.

He's ready, the decision made, everything over but the shouting.

Then it happens: they see the girl.

She's there when Alex pulls on the high beams, illuminated in the bright glare of the Holden's lights. She stands in the middle of the road, perfectly still. Wide-eyed and pale with fear, her left arm thrown forward to protect herself from impact. Alex twists the wheel, knowing that it's helpless. Pleads with her to run as the wheels lock, adrenaline flooding his system as their weight and momentum sets them sliding across the dirt and dust.

Brendan screams. The hammering of hearts. The realization that Alex can't stop it. He knows this as he fights to veer left, the ponderous bulk of the Holden ignoring his desires as physics take over. They slide into her, the pale girl thrown against their bonnet, bouncing off the dusty windscreen with a sickening thump picked up by the stomach more than the ear. She disappears into the darkness behind the car. The Holden slides, tips. Rolls onto its roof and keeps going. Everything is impacts and motion, a tumbling rush towards the trees. They hit with the weight of a cannonball. A delicate bloom of blood on their windshield. Snapped branches, breaking glass.

Their momentum arrested, stopped short by a tree that snaps in two, leaving behind a stubborn trunk large enough to hold them in place. Their roll halts unexpectedly. Alex's head connects with the car window—

Darkness. Nothing. Except the voice, pleading.

Please, stay with me. Please.

Alex comes to when a semi roars down the Landsborough, just a few hundred meters back. The guttural roar of its engine sends a shudder through the Holden. He's still holding the steering wheel in a white-knuckle grip. The Holden is on an angle, the driver's side up resting against the broken tree. Brendan is curled into a ball, arms in front of his face.

Ohmygod, the younger man whispers, over and over like it's a mantra. *Ohmygod. Ohmygod. Ohmygod. Ohmygod.*

Alex fumbles with his seatbelt. Wonders why the semi didn't stop to offer aid.

There's a gash on Brendan's forehead, leaking fluid plastering dark hair against his skull. Pain in Alex's jaw and cheek, a sticky sensation that can only be blood working its way along his neck. Brendan is shaking, rattling with shock.

"You able to move?" Alex says, and Brendan goes still. Voice fading in the question's aftermath.

"We need to get out," Alex says. "Find her."

Brendan doesn't register at first. Alex repeats the request.

Uncouples Brendan's seatbelt, urges his lover free of the Holden and makes his own way out.

The initial step falters, his legs shaky. Alex's forehead stings in the cold night air, a shallow pain that deepens as he pushes himself clear of the vehicle. Brendan has stumbled forward, towards the patch of road illuminated by the sole headlight that survived the moment of impact. Alex casts about, assesses the damage, the stump that halted their momentum and propped them at an angle. He scans the darkness behind them for a body, struggling to comprehend the possibility he's hit someone.

"Hello?" Alex yells. "Can you hear me?"

The only response is the chorus of cicadas, a hesitant restart of their song now the crash is over.

It's a bright night, a waxing moon. No clouds, no light pollution, a mass of stars gathered overhead to observe them. Alex stumbles forward, frantically searching where they've been. The long furrows in the dirt where skidding tires struggled for traction. The broken shards of a shattered headlight litter the red dirt, smashed when they hit the girl. He searches the scrub on both sides of the track, looking for broken branches or some sign of a mangled body.

The shadows are black and inky, giving away nothing. No sign of a victim.

But he hears her, the girl. In the depths of his head. *Please, stay with me. Please.*

"Alex?" Brendan's cry, behind him. A hesitant question, urgent, pleading. Alex turns and looks back, sees Brendan's silhouette as the younger man begins his own search. Alex goes to call out, let Brendan know he's okay. His voice fails, a soft squeak drowned out by the serenity of the cicadas. The pale moon overhead becomes bright and hard. The cicada song grows louder, a monolithic noise. Panic sets in, and Alex abandons the search, stumbling for the car. His body sluggish and weak.

No. Stay with me.

Not a plea. A demand. The world twists and Alex pitches forward, his legs giving out a few meters from the wreckage.

Pain seeps into every part of his existence as he lies there, the dull ache in his head growing sharp tendrils that spread through his neck, his arms, his chest. Panic gives way to terror, a thundering heartbeat, unable to move, his vision swimming as the surroundings refuse to come into focus.

Brendan's shadow falls over him. Alex feels light-headed, his eyes blinking away spots as he stares into the golden headlight. Brendan's cold hand touches his forehead, jerks backwards when it finds blood. "Are you okay?"

Alex grunts, does his best to hold down a trill of nervous laughter. He can't move. His voice is a ragged croak amid the sea of agony overwhelming him.

"We've got to find the girl," he says. "She could be hurt."

Brendan doesn't listen. Brendan never does. He tries to help Alex upwards, back on his feet, but the tendrils of pain solidify into a cohesive, obliterative mass. Alex is a dead weight against the gritty soil. He struggles to choke down a scream.

"Alex?" Brendan's shadow lowers Alex down, voice threaded with worry. "Shit, Alex. What's wrong?"

The girl, Alex says, unsure if the words came out.

The darkness is creeping in now, his consciousness teetering on the edge, threatening to fall backwards into the empty weight of the rocky track. Brendan's footsteps, a soft whisper against the thunder of the cicadas. "There is no girl," he says. "There's nobody there, 'Lex. I can't see her."

Keep looking, Alex says. Or, at least, he thinks he says it. Thinks he gets some version of the words out, to spur Brendan to keep searching. Pain fills his body like a primal scream, so loud even the cicada song fades into the background. Alex can't twist now, can't do anything but hurt. He stares at the full moon, pale-skinned and radiant. A glowing dot he latches onto amid the blackness rushing to drown him.

Keep looking, he says, unsure of what he's hoping for.

Then he hears her: *Stay with me.*

Where are you? Call out. Brendan will come and find you.

I don't want him, she says.

And then the world cants sideways, a spinning impact he doesn't expect. Alex tumbles into the darkness like he's rolling across the hood of a car, the impact snapping bones, tearing muscle, bruising skin.

His eyes shut, clenched against the agony. Against the fear of what's happening to him. Pretending that it's all okay. Feigning control, as he always does, despite the overwhelming pain.

"Open your eyes," she whispers, and Alex obeys. The moon is still there, a pale blot against the starless sky above him. A single, half-crescent of light that cuts through his eyes like steel shrapnel rends flesh.

His body is a broken mass, lying awkward and feeble on a bed of rocks and dirt and leaves. One arm bent backwards, his jaw dislocated. Every cry for help answered by a stab of pain. His hip, fractured. His lungs, filling with blood. Every breath rasps sharp and heavy, drawn in through a mouth of bodily fluids and dirt and fear that he's going to perish.

The part of him that knows this isn't real tries to rationalize with the rest of him.

You could die alone out here, that part of him says. Huddle in pain for hours.

You could die alone out here, it says. But Brendan is with you, somewhere.

You could die alone out here, it says.

Stay with me.

The girl's voice. Responding. Pleading. The raw hope Alex will obey.

Alex senses a presence behind him. Another broken body sprawled on the wilting grass, its quiet moan both wet and dark in the scabrous moonlight. A girl's whimper that Alex is sure belongs to somebody other than Brendan, someone filled with more anger and pain than a city boy like Brendan could ever hold inside.

Over here, Alex thinks. *Brendan, the girl's over here.*

As though Brendan might have missed this. As though either of them could have overlooked an injured woman laying so close to the car. As though thought alone will bring Brendan running.

Alex rolls, forcing his shattered body to move as he searches for the girl, tears streaming as a fresh wave of pain washes through him.

This is death, then. Everything is pale and scabrous, black scrub and jaundiced light. There is no sign of Brendan, no sign of the Holden and its single glaring headlight. Only the road, hollow and lonely. The white crucifix, two bits of wood nailed together, hammered into the crumbly soil of the shoulder to hold a memory in place.

The small figure on the ground, pale and translucent as frost. Cold and so very alone, dying. An awkward arm reaching towards him, trying to take his hand. Pleading with Alex to stay. To descend with her. To share in those final, lonely moments.

He reaches for her, and her touch is bleak. A chill that spreads through pain-wracked limbs like a trail of tears, dulling the jagged roar of broken bones and purple-black bruises.

A pitiful smile of gratitude from her. The sharp teeth, and dark eyes that dominate the pale lines of her face. Eyes that seem to whisper into his soul, a quiet *stay with me* that echoes among the empty hollows of the heart.

If he stays, it will hurt, but it will not hurt that bad.

If he stays, it will be easy. Nothing else need matter but the pain, and the knowledge he'll never be alone.

Alex holds onto the cold, the unspoken desperation. He wraps himself in those two feelings like they're a rug that will ward off danger. Reaches out one hand to caress the girl's head, run his fingers through the night-black strands of hair to comfort her.

The world is pale around them, an unreal forest spun from moonlight and shadow. A lonely place to die, in the early hours of the morning. The victim of drunk friends in a dented ute, bush-bashing to break the monotony of small town life. Unlicensed, underage, making the most of the empty track. Kids that ran when they realized her injuries, afraid of trouble with the cops, convinced no help could save her.

Stay with me, the girl whispers, voice nothing more than a croak after hours of crying and suffering. Her breath scented with wet earth and long-stale blood. Her broken hands clutching at Alex, feeble strength in bloody fingers. He knows how she felt out here, the endless waiting for someone to come. The infinite longing to be free of the pain, a respite from the act of enduring it, clinging to life. Those hours seep beneath the skin: the hoping; the praying; the yearning for an end.

It would be so easy to stay. To nestle beside her and wrap his arms around the broken shell of her body, give up and disappear into the endless night. Comfort her, *it's okay. I'm not going anywhere. I'm staying.*

There are fingers on his arm. Not the girl's touch—stronger warmer.

A ragged voice declaring: "He's mine."

Brendan, Alex whispers, but the words don't come out. His lung good for nothing but wet, unsteady breathing. His heart is a ball of agony, each beat irregular and a little slower than the one that came before it. He'll die here, on the side of the red dirt road. Perish just like the pale girl, broken and alone.

"He's mine, you can't have him." Brendan's voice, soft and clear in the moonlight, and Alex clutches to the life-preserving promise of the claim. The dead girl lurches upwards, broke-angled arms twisting as she reaches out to bind him tighter. Alex's heart wrenches as he struggles to retreat.

"Alex, wake up. I can't do this for you."

The temptation to leave is strong. Set aside the fear and the doubt, the arguments about his trips home, the things Alex refuses to say out loud. Escape the eternal waiting for signs he's a grownup now. Settle into a life with a young dead girl and stay there, always, forever.

"Alex, come back," Brendan says. "Choose me. Please, let her go."

Brendan's not in Alex's field of vision, he hears the voice out in the darkness. Calmer than it should be, trying to lure him home. Alex conjures the image of Brendan: the thin lips, the dark hair, the black nails, and the wry smile. The kisses upon his shoulder, the firm touch of his fingers.

The dead girl objects, a broken jaw attempting words that come out as a low moan. Alex closes his eyes. He focuses on Brendan's voice.

FIVE

"Alex," Brendan says, pleading now, and Alex leverages his eyelids open and stares at the younger man's face. Pale and unreal, like the moon's reflection drifting on dark water. Red-rimmed eyes brimming with tears, haunted by the fear of what might be happening. Brendan, weeping, mascara running. Worried that Alex will leave him, trying to coax him back.

"Hey," Alex whispers, and the world slips into clarity. Brendan kneeling over him, the sky full of stars, the rich smell of leaves and bark and dusty. The tick of the cooling Holden engine, the single headlight shining ahead. No presence beside him, no dead girl clinging to his arm. Just the faint echo of a scream, a lonely cry of grief and loneliness that's already fading.

Alex lies there, pain receding, phantom pains retreating into memory. "I found her," he says, and it still hurts to talk. "I found the girl. She wanted me to go."

Brendan nods, stroking Alex's hair. A gentle gesture, his touch intended to calm. It helps. It feels familiar.

"You almost left me for a girl?" Brendan is trying for a joke, but it doesn't land. Tears glimmer in the corner of his eyes.

The ache is Alex's head is deafening, so violently loud that it threatens to split his skull. His leg splinted, white wood from a roadside crucifix held in place with strips of black velvet, the tattered remains of Brendan's favorite shirt. The sun is creeping over the horizon, the dim gray of pre-dawn shedding a soft light on the overturned Holden. The furrows in the dirt track where they slid and rolled and hit the tree.

"You were so still," Brendan says, sniffling a little.

"It's okay. I'm back," Alex says. "I'm not going away again."

"You were so *still*," Brendan repeats, a pleading note in his voice. Not game to ask what he really wants, but Alex knows. He can hear it in there.

"Shh," Alex says. Weak, but attempting to comfort. A return to his role as the reasonable one.

Brendan's eyes leak, more eyeliner smudging his cheeks. Alex tries to wipe the tears, letting the pain recede like a departing tide, drifting out on the receding darkness. Each tear dims the roar in his head, brings him closer to a reality with no injury, no dead girl, no plea to stay and salve a loneliness that can never, truly, be salved.

Brendan hikes back to the highway. Tasked with flagging down a truck or a car, getting a call put into the Charleville ambulance. Folks rise early, in this part of the world. The main roads are never so empty as they look when you're driving alone.

Alex puts a hand against the white splints, the broken crucifix that served as a memorial without name or date. A marker: bad things happened here.

He breathes deep and exhales. The morning air is cold and crisp and new. He smiles, despite the pain, and awaits Brendan's return with help. With an ambulance and doctors, with painkillers and a proper cast to keep his leg in place.

It's not so bad, he tells himself. Existing. Life. It's not so bad having someone to love you, even if it's just for a while.

He breathes in. He breathes out. Focuses on rise and fall beneath his ribs, the slow inflation of the lungs. It ends up hurting a little less every time he does it. In. Out. Accepting the change in rhythm. Still painful, but not so bad now. A reminder that flesh can heal.

Moment by moment, things get better.

Moment by moment, he stays.

RULE 34

They are not the creatures they were, if you pay attention to the legends. We have that drilled into us, after we're recruited, long before Carter lets a newcomer place fingers upon the keyboard. He wants to make sure we're prepared what's coming; barely understands the impossibility of the task.

We've got many names for them around the office: jinn; genies; the demons of a smokeless flame. Carter prefers to call them Entities, pronounces it so you can hear the capital E, but he isn't present long enough for his preferences to matter.

Carter is an asshole, and tight-lipped with those in his employ. What the floor team know, we learned from Shamil, who works three desks over from mine. He believed in the Entities before Carter recruited him, brought his beliefs into the lab where the rest of us toiled at the keyboards. This affords him the status of an expert when we muse about the creatures we hunt.

Because of Shamil we recognize the Entities have free will, that God will judge them as he judges humanity when the end of all things arrives. And it's because of Shamil that we have theories about the jinn's withdrawal into the net, disappearing into a frontier of electrons and fiber optic cables after centuries inhabiting isolated mountains, clouds, and deep trenches of the oceans. Because of him we have arguments about how they ended up there, whether they retreated to internet of their own volition or were imprisoned there by a third party, as human mystics once captured jinn in lamps with occult seals.

Shamil was born in Los Angeles; spent his teenage years in Denver. The only kid in his class to study the Koran and memorize the Canticles of Solomon, who tamed the jinn and counted them among his servants, holding them in bondage until his death.

This, too, affords Shamil a measure of authority when discussing the jinn, for he understands what it is to relocate against your will and adapt to new surrounds. He tells tales that suggest Carter is not mad; that perhaps he truly can capture the Entities we chase and force them to attend to a master's wishes.

I remain unconvinced, but I do enjoy the stories. They provide moments of respite amid the work Carter demands of us.

We spend our days on the internet, dreaming of things that shouldn't exist. Bizarre porn; unexpected fetishes; weird little sites that serve no real purpose beyond their own existence. The kinds of dreams that make you wonder, "Who in hell puts this online?"

Except we don't wonder, down in Carter's laboratory. We know, 'cause Carter makes sure we know. Because he lays it all out on the very first day, before you're ever introduced to the rest of the lab, and he'll remind you every time he sees you, however short his visit.

"Rule Thirty-Four," he says, "that's how we'll chase the bastards down."

Rule 34 exists because the jinn make their home on the internet. Any fetish you can imagine, they will provide.

Sit at your keyboard, with your mind clear. Let your fingers rest upon the keys, the worn squares of plastic with missing letters courtesy of years spent punching out word after word. Let your attention wander.

It starts with a simple indulgence. A fetish for women caught in the rain, their damp clothing welded to their body by the torrential downpour, or a penchant for feet with polydactyl traits, supernumerary toes displayed with pride. Men with octopus tentacles where their right arm should be, each specimen arranged naked, supine, and resplendent on a sandy beach. You don't expect to find anything, but the web provides it anyway. There are sites full of pictures. Communities to join. People who seem to share your interest, willing to help you take it further. Porn sites. Slash fic. Secret Tumblr feeds and dark web enclaves, unapologetic in their content. If you're smart, you'll back off and forget about what you've seen. Realize there are some temptations one shouldn't succumb too, even at an introductory subscription price of $2.99.

If you're not smart, you'll go deeper down the rabbit hole. You pit your will against the jinn and the illusions they can offer you, each of them darker than the one that came before it, but still so very sweet and tempting.

Some people—strong willed and conscious of their boundaries—recognize it's time to cease engaging with the jinn.

Those of us on Carter's team, we kept falling. Entertained desires so specialized only the jinn could cater to them. Called in sick to day jobs, so we could stay online. Gave up work, so we could better explore our desires.

We'd all be falling still if the boss hadn't found us and offered us an alternative path.

Carter has a plan to capture the jinn. When our team finds a likely site, we alert his squad of hackers. They go to work locking down the internet, trying to seize hold of a figment as the jinn slips through fiber optic relays and disappears from the local nodes.

Some days we get bored, staring at the screens. Days when any fetish we can dream up seems tame and not worth seeking. On those days, we theorize about the jinn and what happens next. Shamil remains adamant that capture is possible, despite the prevailing theory that the jinn are light made sentient, their physical forms as illusory as the manifested fantasies that play out on our monitors.

Some mornings it all seems a waste of time: jinn;

pornography; Carter's long-term plans. They've slipped through our net too many times, placated desires we barely conceived of until they revealed themselves online.

And despite Carter's warnings, it's always a surprise. The jinn were never content to grant wishes, even in the stories. They twisted every desire, sought loopholes to exploit. They held up a facet of your own inclinations and made it seem darker, harder to deny.

You see things that unsettle you, in this job, not least 'cause you find yourself aroused. You stop looking in the mirror, because it makes the days easier. I gave up mirrors a few weeks back; Shamil is starting familiar arguments, suggesting that he'll be next.

But the money's outstanding, so we sit and get paid for a thing done gratis: scour the net, getting specific, trying to prove Rule 34 wrong.

We search for a digital footprint in the landscape of our desires.

LOCAL HEROES

THINGS YOU CAN'T PAY BACK

Gold Coast summers are a little slice of Hades on earth. Endless weeks of scorching days and humid nights, the temperature pushing forty on the Celsius scale. A punishing, sweltering heat that makes you regret being alive, the moisture thick enough to chew up and spit out if you're willing to risk prolonged activity. Then the tourists descend, a plague of biblical proportions: on the beaches; on the streets; constant treks across the mountains and constant theme parks. Tourists in the fucking Hell Bar, obliging me to deal with them every damned night.

The holiday crowds reminded me why I first left all those years ago. Those self-indulgent fuckers got me think real hard about fleeing the Coast again, even if staying put was safer for a man in my situation.

I was thinking all those kinds of thoughts the morning Holly Langford cornered me at my latest safe-house. I climbed out of a cab at four AM, crossed the sun-blasted grass that masqueraded as a yard. Didn't spot Langford parked on the front step, dreadlocks pooled around her skinny arse. Killing time with a Winnie Blue she'd smoked down to the filter.

I stopped short and wondered how the fuck I'd missed her. It wasn't like Langford blended, not in the white-bread coastal suburbs pressed up against the shoreline. Six-three and stalk-thin, piercings through nose, lip and brow. Tattoos covering exposed skin long since worn to leather by hard living. Some of that ink I knew real well, tether marks that connected Langford to the other world and channeled the raw stuff of magic into our dimension. Other tats were decorative, or camouflage to keep the unwary from recognizing her as a sorcerer.

Langford sucked on her cigarette and eyed my approach. "Took your time."

"Didn't know about the meeting."

"You're still late." Langford exhaled a final cloud of smoke and flicked the butt across the yard. She hauled herself upright with the cast-iron railing and looked me over, blocking my path to the door.

I halted at the bottom stop. "Thought I gave you the spare key?"

"No smoking apartment," Langford said. "And it would have fucked your wards. Of course, that would be a fucking a mercy killing, way you handle defenses. There's a real strong argument for establishing protection that can actually keep threats out—you might try it sometime."

"And live in a world where you don't show up, unannounced? Inconceivable."

"Funny." Langford stepped away to allow me access the flat. "Just open the door, eh?"

I stifled a yawn and obeyed. Twelve hours working the bar meant I wasn't inclined towards visitors, but Langford wouldn't give a crap. Refuse the people you owe debts to in my line of work and bad things happen, especially when you're in so deep that paying it off was a pipe dream.

My flat was a bare bones operation. One bedroom, ensuite bathroom, a small kitchenette. Habits of a lifetime meant I didn't keep much there. A handful of clothes, four second-hand books, enough weapons to hold off a demon attack if I got very lucky. A go-bag, tucked beneath the bed, ready bail on the place in a hurry if the situation demanded.

Langford flopped into the leather arm-chair while I headed to the kitchenette. The flat came with a bare minimum of cooking gear—one plate, two forks, a knife, three teaspoons. The kettle was an old, stove-top job barely up to boiling water, but I unearthed the last clean mugs and set them both on the bench.

Langford rolled a cigarette and kicked a heel against the coffee table. "You look okay, considering."

"If you say so. Nescafe or English breakfast?"

"Tea." Langford touched a fingertip to the cancer stick and flame bloomed at the end. My wards surged, fighting to tamp down the flow of magic, but they weren't up to the job. Langford was an experienced witch, highly trained and older than she looked. My own skills ran in a different direction and relied on 9mm bullets and a low-key gift for sensing the Gloom.

I poured hot water over a Lipton bag. "How you take it?"

"Black. Two sugar."

Langford studied my moves as I spooned things out, checking for signs the eye-patch was giving me trouble. Her lack of subtlety gave me the shits. "Depth perception was a bitch, the first three weeks, but I'm learning to adapt."

She perched on the edge of the chair like a falcon, ready to swoop in. I made the fucking tea, handed her the cup. Langford took it, sipped it. Nodded her satisfaction.

The apartment seemed to bother her though. "I see you're settling in for the long haul?"

"It is what it is. Old habits."

Langford tapped a finger against her occipital bone. "The eye isn't—"

"I'm doing okay." I dropped an ashtray in front of Langford, went to claim my mug. Then we stared at each other, waiting, assessing. That wouldn't end well for me. You don't win staring matches against a witch.

Langford ashed her cigarette and grinned. "I've got a situation."

"Right," I said. "The fun kind, or the other?"

"The other. You'd call it an old-school type of party."

Which meant Langford had need of my former profession, and the skills picked up before I managed a bar frequented by creatures who go bump in the night. I took a deep breath and nodded. "Okay."

"No questions?"

"Not how this works. You require a contract done, I do it."

"It's not—" she hesitated. "Shit, Murphy, I'm not fucking Roark, demanding you jump on command because the crusade is all that matters."

"Debts get paid off. First rule of the game."

Langford raised an eyebrow. Truth is, I would have taken the job even without the debt. Hell Bar wasn't a bad gig, but I'd spent the better part of a decade hunting things that go bump in the night—demons and warlocks and rogue entities from the Gloom. Not the smartest deal for a mortal, but practice ensured I got pretty good and my boss Danny picked up the slack.

The Hell Bar was just the stop-gap after that gig crashed down around me, courtesy of a hit Danny Roark and I fucked up down Adelaide way. Bar service and handling payroll didn't exactly satisfy me, not after all those years of taking down monsters too dangerous to leave walking free.

"The job," I said. "Tell me."

Langford screwed up her face, stared at her mug of tea. She wasn't comfortable giving orders yet. "I got a friend, Gareth Cottee. He works up at the university. Good bloke, once you get past his talent for talking shit and insistence on poking his nose where he shouldn't. Took it upon himself to monitor some local Other, up Brisbane way. Says it's reaching a point where there's a dark influence in need of curbing. I never bothered policing that crap, but since you're around and looking for things to do…"

"You require a trigger man."

Langford worried at a knuckle. "Maybe."

"All I have to hear," I said. "Tell me about the target."

Langford tossed a flyer onto the coffee table. It promised a thing called Rampage Pro was heading back to the Nundah Community Hall, headlined by Rocky Malice versus Eddie Coltrane. Glossy photographs of the two men sat underneath the logo. Malice wore black trunks and painted his face like Bruce Lee's kid in The Crow. Coltrane was a chubby bloke, the fold of his gut hanging over his jeans, greasy hair dangling over his Cheshire-Cat grin.

The other names on the card were equally improbable, but at

least they spared me the photographs. One name circled in red pen: Ketch.

"You're kidding, right?"

"I'm not."

"Pro-wrestling?"

"I don't pick where the target works."

My eyes dropped to the flyer. "So long as your friend ain't the fucker in the face-paint."

"That's not Cottee's scene. He's more an observer."

"By observer you mean fan?"

"Researcher. Specializes in semiotics and cultural studies up at uni." She waved her hand towards the door, like the campus was just outside. "Pop culture as modern mythology, all that kind of bullshit."

"He knows magic?"

"Nope. Interested amateur. Sufficient knowledge to find trouble, but—"

She stopped, took a short breath. "Look, he knows stuff. Enough that I take his concerns on board. Isn't the first time Gareth's mentioned this problem, but he's getting a little urgent about it. Insists I check out the show and give my two cents on proceedings."

"So we're going?"

Langford grinned. "You're kidding, right? It's a goddamn wrestling show."

A bunch of things clicked into place for me. "Ah," I said. "So I'm your proxy."

Langford tapped the side of her nose. "Investigate. Assess. Come back and get me if Cottee's stumbled across a big-bad in need of killing."

I picked up the flyer again. Saturday night.

"Best see if Price can manage the bar for me. Seems I'll be busy."

GOOD THINGS

Gareth Cottee proved to be a tall, heavy guy built like a wheelie bin: long frame, thick shoulders, plenty of girth to go along with them. He showed up dressed in a dark-green Ninja Turtle's tee and camouflage-pattern Chucks which had seen better days. The knot of the flannel shirt tied around his waist disappeared beneath the overhang of his gut, and a thatch of lank hair and untamed beard invited speculation about whether his neck existed underneath. He parked an SUV at the top of the Broadbeach mall and bounded over to my park bench with the eagerness of a hyperactive spaniel. "So you're Keith Murphy?" he said. "I've heard brilliant things about you, sir."

Those weren't words I'm used to hearing from strangers. "Brilliant?"

"Holly speaks highly of you, says we owe you big for stopping some kind of apocalypse." He nodded enthusiastically. "I make a point of paying attention when she mentions contacts like that. It's a rarity, since she stopped taking an active interest in—"

Shit. I cut him off. "Mister Cottee, I—"

"Gareth, please."

"Gareth, this isn't—"

"Oh. Yes, of course. Say no more." Gareth Cottee winked and broke out an eager grin. The intensity of his good humour infused his gaze, a stark contrast to his large frame. Like glimpsing an unfocused-but-brilliant intelligence in the eyes of a wooly mammoth. His attention darted to the next idea: "Discretion. Discretion. One reason Holly never deployed in the field. Never stopped me, you understand, but—"

"Gareth?"

He raised his eyebrows.

"We're running late," I said. "Perhaps we should get moving?"

"Oh," he said. "Right. Of course."

It's a long drive to Brisbane, from my neck of the woods. Longer with a man like Cottee at the wheel, working his mouth at ten clicks a minute while he wove through the highway traffic. He shared things at a pace that left me feeling dizzy: thirty-four years old, lecturing in cultural studies; interested in folklore and semiotics and other shit I barely understood, which is how he fell in with Langford in the early days of his degree. Held forth on the artistic importance of the Bee Gees as we took the tunnel to Brisbane's north side.

I stopped listening, chimed in with a nod or a-huh every few minutes. I'd worked with men talked compulsively before, back when me and Danny Roark still traveled as a team. You learn the art of faking interest and getting ready for a job.

I'd like to say it taught me I shouldn't dismiss guys who deployed conversation to burn off nervous energy, but truth is, Gareth Cottee gave me the shits. By the time we hit Nundah, I was daydreaming about leaving him in a ditch.

We pulled up out front of the Nundah Community Hall. Dinky little building nestled up against a cricket pinch, a handful of pine trees marking out the edge of the car-park crammed to capacity. A small crowd queued up against the wall, standing by for doors to open. Maybe two hundred people, all walks of life: fathers with their kids, out for an evening's entertainment; small clusters of goth-faced teens in black jackets and fishnets; sullen men in their thirties who could have raided Cottee's wardrobe. Island boys, dressed in baggy jean and tight tees, tattoo sleeves on display as they talked shit from their place in the queue. A couple of obvious gym-bunnies, muscles pumped up like balloons. Lots of them talking like they knew wrestlers personally, a friend and family crowd.

Cottee and I fell in at the rear. He twitched with nervous energy, eager to be inside. He said: "You've not done this before, right?"

I raised an eyebrow. "This?"

"A wrestling show."

"Not here for the wrestling."

"Yeah," Cottee said. "Your enthusiasm shows."

I shrugged. "Always struck me as ten kinds of stupid."

Cottee nodded. "I get that. Heard it a lot, when I first started writing papers about it. Like most things, it gets more interesting when you pay close attention."

"I'll take your word on that," I said, hoping to stall the conversation.

Turns out, I wasn't that lucky. The doors swung open, and we shuffled forward, tickets in hand, and Cottee blathered on. "I got interested in my undergraduate, reading Roland Barthes. He wrote an essay about the semiotics of a wrestling match, the way each man embodies notions of heroism and villainy," he said. "All this? It's one of the last true passion plays left in Western culture. The hero suffers for no other reason than embodying the act of suffering, the villain who cheats does so because ritual demands a despicable deed. The masses cheer, and hate, and empathize on cue."

We shuffled inside, got our first look at the sagging ring. It didn't inspire confidence, but the hall buzzed with conversations as the crowd searched for seats. "So," I said. "You're a fan?"

"Certainly, but never *just* that. I became hooked studying the modern incarnation of the sport. After that, there was…"

Cottee's smile wilted as he trailed off. He pointed to a spot in the back row, close to the exit. "I'll be honest with you, Mister Murphy. I'm surprised it took this long for an entity of the Gloom to embrace the possibilities. The wrestling ring is a microcosm for studying the Other—every man who steps into that squared circle draws power from being part of the story, transformed into a symbol of something greater than himself. It doesn't play with subtlety and metaphor, it transforms men into avatars of good and evil, then asks the audience to believe. Given the nature of magic, as I understand it…"

The heat in the small building was oppressive and thick with humidity. The buzz of the crowd rattled against my skull, too many people crammed into a cramped space. Too much power gathered in one place, the Gloom responding to concentrated belief. "Okay," I said. "If you're correct, that could be bad."

The grin returned. "Bad's understating things by a considerable degree," Cottee said. "Assuming my theories about the Gloom is accurate, there's no better place than a wrestling company for an entity to hide and build up power without being noticed. It's ritualized, highly symbolic, and people disregard it as a sideshow unworthy of attention."

"Still not convinced there's anything more than play-acting going on in there."

"Not play-acting, iconography." Cottee gestured toward the ring. "Magic's founded on simple semiotics, just like everything else. One thing stands in for another, the symbols connected to esoteric meanings, the signified and the referent drawing power from the signifier. You learn to decode them and poof"—he snapped his fingers in front of my nose—"magic. A stage isn't a ring, a movie villain is not a wrestling heel. The space shapes the performance, re-codes the symbols in different ways."

The fervor creeping into the academic's voice worried me. "You know they're not really fighting, right?"

Cottee sighed, rolled his eyes. "If any of this happened for real, Mister Murphy, trust me, none of this would be a problem."

FIRST FALL TO A FINISH

The seven-thirty kick-off arrived closer to eight, lights dimming to quiet the fans. The opening match pitted two scrawny rookies against each other. Both eighteen, nineteen years old, still with the undersized look young athletes have—sleek and muscled, but not bulked out. They lasted five painful minutes. Bad holds, sloppy punches, a quick gouge to the eye by the smaller of the two to get the pinfall. A handful of people booed the victor, the rest of us just sat there. Cottee lapsed into quiet commentary, unearthing the pattern underlying the fight, a rhythm and a ritual designed give meaning to every move and counter.

The second match featured another skinny youngster, all sinew and bone. He squared off against an evil-looking fucker with a beer gut and a perpetual scowl. Beer Gut slapping the hell out of the kid, raising welts on his chest. It earned more sympathy than either guy in the first bout, and the crowd erupted when the kid connected with a roundhouse kick and picked up the three-count.

We made it to the fourth match before I excused myself, found my way to the concession stand where a crew of older women were serving hotdogs and cans of Pepsi. I paid for one of each, absconded to an isolated spot behind the rows of seating. The slap of flesh on flesh echoed off the concrete walls, but my position offered a brief respite from Cottee's rambling monolog.

I devoured the food mechanically, my hotdog cold in the middle. The first three matches had the virtue of being short, despite their other flaws. The fourth ticked into its twelfth minute as I finished eating and showed no sign of ending. I headed outside and dialed Langford's number. "Cottee's a freakin' lunatic."

"I hear you."

"He ever shut up?"

"Nope. Told you he worked for a university?"

"I believe you. The man's been lecturing non stop since we left the coast."

"Gareth's a little weird, but that doesn't mean he's wrong. Get back in there and pay attention."

I returned to the hall just in time for the short intermission. Cottee found me against the back wall. "First match back," he said.

"What?"

"Keating versus Hangman Ketch. The one you got to see," he said. "We're done here, afterwards. I'm either right, or you tell Langford I'm full of shit and my credibility takes a hit. I may be an opinionated asshole, but I don't do this to torture you."

More self-awareness than I'd expected from the man. It earned him a little slack. When he returned to his seat, I followed him. They announced the fifth match fight after the lights dimmed, a tuxedo-clad announcer hyping the fans into a frenzy.

I heaved a deep breath. A final round and I was in the clear.

And then the demon turned up.

I'd known plenty of demons, killed my fair share of them. This one walked like a predator, weight on the balls of his feet. An ebony forelock draped over a gaunt face rendered in stark, monochromatic make-up. Bone-pale skin, kohl-rimmed stare, lips marked with black ink that bled into the white flesh around his mouth. A noose hung around his neck, the knot dangling between his pectorals, and he rippled with lean muscle.

Dark, shimmering eyes studied the crowd, ignoring their jeers. I wished I could sink into the wall, slide away from that stare without being noticed. The demon climbed into the ring and roared, showed off teeth filed into sharp points. The fans hated him, right on cue, and Ketch's low-laughter mocked them all as he lounged against the ropes, one hand lifting the end of the noose and stuck out his tongue in a vulgar mockery of a hanging.

His opponent was older, a tall blonde with the physique of a front-row forward, all jaw-line and shoulders and focus. The guy you'd expect to dismantle a leaner, sleeker opponent, and you'd be disappointed. The demon moved fast, all grace and quick bursts of power. They locked up, arms gripping one-another's elbows, and started forcing each other around the ring.

"Jesus," I said.

"Yeah," Cottee said, "he's something, isn't he?"

Something wasn't the word I'd use. Outright bloody terrifying hit closer to the mark. Every demon I've met was some kind of dangerous, but they only crossed over from the Gloom when they found a mortal host. Relied heavily on corruption and wheedling, right up to the point they subsumed the host's memories and eliminated the human spirit.

That took time, and if you're lucky, a little humanity stained the demonic soul. But I doubted the fucker inside the ring ever felt the sting of earthly emotions.

They ran through Cotte's ritual movements, wrestler and demon working in unison: shine, heat, come back, cut-off, finish. Cottee explained every step along the way, made sure I understood why it was happening. The shine saw the good guy take an early upper hand, demonstrating victory was possible against the superior skill of his opponent. Heat came after an illegal move, delivered control to the heel for a stretch. The good guy takes advantage of a moment of hubris, rallies as he makes a fast-paced combat. A cheap shot provides a hiccup, then everything is fury and fortune until the final pinfall.

Even with the knowledge it wasn't real, Ketch's offense stopped my breathing ever time he landed a blow. The impact of every powerslam vibrated through the pit of my stomach. "Wait," Cottee said, "it'll pass, soon enough."

The end followed a thumb to the eye, blinding the good guy and setting him up for pain. The demon hovered, lips curved into a cruel line. It soaked up crowd's derision, feeding on their hatred, and I caught a glimpse of everything Gareth Cottee fretted about. Ketch elbowed his opponent and picked the reeling wrestler up, prepared to plunge the other guy brain-first into the mat. The aura of menace around Ketch grew thicker, stronger. I could taste it, thick and bloody, roiling against the back of my throat.

"Shit," I said, and Cottee nodded.

Ketch spiked the rangy blonde into the canvas, all the impact focused on head and neck. The blond kid sprawled, limp and boneless, still as death while the demon covered his shoulders. I held my breath, fingers drifting towards the gun holstered beneath my jacket. Cottee laid a warning hand against my wrist. "Wait," he said. "Just give them a moment."

The referee counted off the victory, count falling to the canvas three times. Hangman Ketch looped his noose over his opponent, pulled it tight. Stood and smirked at the crowd, before stalking out of the ring. His exit took him so close to us I could see the beads on sweat on his bare chest. He lingered, flipping the bird to jeering kids the next row down. Then Ketch looked over and flashed a mocking wink right at Gareth Cottee.

Two ambulance officers came to remove the other wrestler. They lifted him to his feet, lugged him backstage. I let them get through another bout, then abandoned my chair and went outside.

STEPS

The worst part about flying solo is making all the decisions. Me and Roark, we'd been a partnership, but the Old Man took the lead on picking jobs. He knew the terrain, and he understood magic. I treated my ability to pierce the veils of the Gloom as a hindrance and focused on wet work. Now he's gone and all the conclusions were mine to come to. And scary as Hangman Ketch seemed in the ring, he might still be a character. The demon behind the wrestler bore further investigation.

The second worst part of flying solo was taking responsibility for passive surveillance. I got the address of the Rampage Wrestling School from Cottee, staked out the entrance for two days before I latched onto Ketch heading in for a session. He dressed down for training. No make up, sweatpants and a singlet, a pair of beat-up docs on his feet as he climbed out of the car. I hunched low in my rented hatchback, waited for him to emerge. Tailed him for the next couple of hours, tracked Ketch to his home.

He rented a duplex by the river in West End, one of the streets that went under in the last flood. The address gave me enough to track the demon's host through Facebook, get the name that appeared on his license. Course, from what I'd seen, Toby Vennis was just another character, a human being who'd been real way back when, but the demon inside him ate all that away, left behind nothing but a shell and some attitude.

I dialed Langford's number from the car. "Well, your friend Cottee definitely found something."

Langford met the news with silence on her end. Then: "You're kidding."

"Nope. We got a kid, maybe twenty-three years old, any semblance of his mortal half long gone from the looks of him. Whatever shit Cottee's rambling 'bout with symbols and wrestling, turns out he may not be full of crap."

"Damn," Langford said. "The demon, it's—"

"Not done a thing, so far as I can see, except perform and train and hang around his house. That's the part that worries me. All that power, no real direction."

"You want to go in?"

"Not yet. But it's coming."

"Keep on it." Lanford blew a slow, weary sigh. "I trust you to make the call here, Murphy."

"Never been my strong suite."

Langford hung up, and I dug in. Drank the bottled water that came with the rental and settled in for the long haul.

There's a process when eliminating a demon. A lot of it requires a shit-ton of patience and the willingness to lie low and avoid detection. That's how you figure out what defenses they've got in place, from magical wards to booby traps that'll blow your damn fingers off if you pick the wrong lock. I'd encountered both on the job before, back when I first worked my way up the food chain. The longer a demon's been around, the more it's settled into its host, the more dangerous they are.

After you've got the defenses down, you start in on the pattern. Figure out the safest places to hit them when you want to avoid detection. Plot where you hide out when the job's done, since most dead demons just look like human corpses, and the cops ain't buying the defense that you killed seemingly ordinary citizens for the good of humanity. It's half the reason folks in my position allowed certain entities to keep walking around, if they limit themselves to the kind of bad shit that doesn't cross a line.

My problem became predicting when and how the demon inside Hangman Ketch might cause harm. The asshole maintained a small, focused routine: he woke, he trained, he prepared for the next wrestling gig. That lack of engagement served as the first sign I needed to take him out, because even demons need to pay rent if they want to blend in.

Ketch wasn't paying his way off local shows or teaching at a school full of undersized rookies, which meant he took shortcuts somewhere. And any entity of the Gloom who defaults to shortcuts is nothing but trouble in the long run.

The surveillance of a target usually lasted four weeks. I tagged team the job with Langford after the first three, focused on the physical aspects of Ketch's existence while she handled the occult stuff. Met up with her fourteen days later, in the McDonalds down in Palm Beach, close to my safe house. Langford ordered a couple of shitty cheeseburgers and a large coke. I opted a black coffee, sat down to wait. Let her eat for a stretch before we started.

"Cottee says there's another wrestling show coming next week," Langford said. There were hollow pockets beneath her eyes, dark and sleepless. She didn't look over, but idle fingers twisted her eyebrow ring while she contemplated the problem. "Based on what I've seen, we want him eliminated before that happens."

I nodded. Drank my coffee. "He still done nothing worth killing him over."

She hesitated, cheeseburger in hand. "Yeah."

"You're leaning towards doing it, just to be on the safe side?"

Langford bit into the burger. Spoke with her mouth full. "Cottee thinks it's necessary. My gut says the same. You?"

"You helped me save the goddamn world. I owe you."

"Your point?"

"My opinion doesn't come into this once you've decided." I sipped my coffee and tried to ignore the shrieks of young children two booths down. "I do wonder why Cottee gets to decide. He doesn't seem like a guy who inspires that kind of faith or loyalty."

"And yet, here we are. Preparing to do the job." Langford unwrapped her third burger, bit into it. Chewed and swallowed. "Cottee's rarely wrong about things. When he says something needs killing…"

"Like I said, just thought it was odd."

"Okay. Noted. Now, consider this." Langford gestured with two-thirds of a cheeseburger. "If any other demon figured out this trick, started using it as a way of helping others strip away their human half a little faster…"

"Yeah. I get it. Bad news for all humanity."

"So we take Ketch out?"

"You don't need to ask."

She pushed a notebook across the table, along with a pencil. "Good. Let's get a plan together. I want this done before the next show hits and the asshole gets another hit of energy."

FORTIFIED

It was hot, the night we set aside to kill Ketch. Langford worked from the back of the van, setting up the ritual that would break down the demon's wards. Me in the front, watching his duplex, leaving sweaty marks on the fake-leather upholstery. The air thick with incense and oppressive humidity, the moon a pale sliver and the streetlights on his street flickering as we waited. Technology and magic have never been a strong combination. Magic flows out of the Gloom, tainted by the shadows there. No lights on in Ketch's home, although I doubted he needed them.

It wasn't much of a place. I figure the kid who'd been Ketch rented it, before he got possessed; semi-furnished, cheap, and perched on a steep slope, the drive little more than a breakneck drop between the roadside and the door. Stubby palms filled the cramped yard and burnt-orange brick walls secured things to the hillside, a desperate attempt to keep soil erosion from sweeping the duplex away. Big windows gave me multiple points of entry, even if they were likely to be loud. I unearthed a SIG, a knife, and a set of lock picks, kept watch while Langford completed her work.

"We're good." Langford settled in the centre of her circle, crossed her legs, and closed her eyes. I slipped free of the van, whispered a short spell to discourage attention as I covered the two blocks between us and Ketch's home. I edged closer to the duplex, counted down from five hundred. The air hummed as I sidled towards the front entrance, goosebumps prickling my arm as Langford's ritual interacted with the first round of wards. I crouched low and worked my picks into the locks, prodded the tumblers until they clicked. Stepped inside before anyone noticed —you can trust magic to cover your tracks, a little, but there's no point taking unnecessary risks. I eased the door shut behind me, quiet as a breath.

This seams of moonlight pried their way in beneath the heavy drapes of a long, narrow lounge I blinked, adapting to the changed light. Kept still and hoped the lingering effects of Langford's spell would keep my scent obscured. I knew the layout of the duplex, courtesy of city plans: two bedrooms to the left, after leaving to the lounge; a small kitchen and dining space on the rear, heading right. Enough room to swing a cat, but if your balance was off the kitty would end up with a concussion. The chewy stink of rotting meat wafted from the garage. The frisson of unravelling magic filled the air with an ozone scent. The soft splash of tap-water, up and round the corner. Ketch lived alone, near as we could tell. I held my breath, edged closer.

He stood at the sink, filling a glass. Boxers only, in the muggy night heat, the muscled lines of his frame silhouetted against the open window. Head low, attention foggy thanks to Langford's magic. I took aim at the broad back and the SIG kicked three times. Two in the chest, one in the skull. Standard operating procedure, whether you're killing men or monsters. Ketch pitched forward, sprawled across his kitchen bench. Didn't move for the space of ten seconds, which was long enough to get me curious.

I approached the body, SIG raised to keep him covered.

Big fucking mistake.

Ketch lashed out, whipping his arm around to smash the tumbler of water against my cheek. The combination of impact, fragile glass, and cheekbone didn't work out too good on my end. Exploding glassware ripped through my face, my blind side a mess of hot blood and sharp pain. Ketch twisted himself upright, a stump of broken glass clenched in his right fist.

The world slowed to a crawl as a fresh wave of adrenaline hit. Gave me all the time I needed to register my mistake. I'd nailed Ketch clean with chest shots, but the headshot creased the skull instead of penetrating bone. Bloody enough to seem effective, but the shot did none of the messy damage to the brain that put a demonic host out for good. The demon would just shut down the pain impulses, force the body to keep moving until the flesh tore itself apart.

Ketch launched his bulk at me, dark blood streaming from his chest. I was already scrambling backwards, trying to get the space to plug him with the SIG and put him down. Ketch blocked my attempt to bring the gun up, slammed me against the wall with a strength no human could ever match. I groped for the knife sheathed at the small of my back, stuck it into his flank as Ketch closed on me. Steel dug into muscle, did just as little as the bullet wounds. Ketch fired a punch at my head that went through the drywall after I ducked to the left.

"You're Cottee's friend," Ketch hissed. "Recognise your scent."

I don't work up-close, not if I can avoid it. I put a round in his leg, tried to slow him down. Didn't work. He came after me, nails elongating into talons that raked at my wrist and face. Ketch latched on and wrenched sideways, hammering my fist against the wall. Pain lurched up my arm and numb fingers dropped the SIG. I got lucky, wrested the knife free of his side. Held it,, in my left hand as I jabbed and gave ground.

Ketch leapt at me, hit me with the blunt force of his shoulder. Knocked me to the floor while he kept his feet. The first kick caught me high, right under the armpit. The second, in the soft parts of my flank, just shy of the place where the ribs would protect me. Both hurt like getting bludgeoned with a sledge, took the fight right out of me.

The third kick hammered me in the skull, bounced my head off kitchen linoleum. The pain in my wrist didn't bother me, after that.

Nothing really bothered me at all.

HEAT

Ketch threw water into my face and I came too, spluttering, desperately fighting to return to the painless darkness. Awake meant acknowledging physical discomfort. My wrist hurt. My cheek hurt. Cold liquid dripped from my nose.

I wasn't dead, which surprised me, but the good news ended there. He'd tied me to an office chair, beside an archaic desk and laptop. Wrists taped to the arms, feet hanging free. Ketch perched on the edge of his couch, lights turned on. Up close, his features were bone-white and ugly, the fluorescent globes giving him a wan, sallow appearance. Lips pulled away from sharp teeth, yellow and stained with stringy lines of drool. A smile. "Your pulse just shifted," Ketch said. "Don't bother trying to pretend you're not awake."

I blinked a few times, lolled my head backwards. Ketch leaned back, showed off the puckered scar-tissue where my first two bullets had caught him. My jaw set, and I regretted it. Pain radiated through my face. "You should be dead."

"And yet, I'm not." Ketch scratched at the healing wounds. "Odds are your little wizard fucked up, or you're not as good as I'd heard. You've got a reputation, killer, after all that shit went down. The local boogie-men are all a-twitter about your presence. Nobody really trusts you, working at your bar. They show up to keep an eye out, waiting for you to fuck up."

I wanted to nod, but I didn't. That way lay pain. I retreated into stillness, matched the demon's gaze. It was one of Roark's rules: hold on to your cool, work the situation. Talk it through until you get an opening. "Seems like your kind need more to gossip about, if all you've got is me."

He punched me in the mouth, put his weight behind. Difficult to do when you're perched on a couch, but Ketch tagged me hard enough that the office chair did a bunny-hop. I rolled backwards a few inches before the drag of my feet slowed things down. I could taste blood, my whole face burning.

"Don't mistake the fact you live for a good thing," Ketch said.

"Noted."

"I'm not a patient man," he declared, and I sucked in a short, desperate breath.

"Ceased being a man at all, second you got possessed."

Ketch nodded. He liked that. "Nor are you, these days."

"You figure?"

"I figure. When a two-bit killer heads to the Gloom, stops himself an apocalypse, my kind figure all kinds of things. When he cuts a deal that keeps him alive, every demon pays attention. We let each other know there's a big damn hero on the block, that it's time to step wary if you're doing wrong." Ketch darted in, clawed hands clamping down on my forearms. Pressed his face real close to mine. "I'm no not fond of a wary existence, hero. It makes me irritable."

I flinched, despite myself. Screwed my good eye shut, waiting for the next punch. Instead, I got treated to his warm breath against my cheek, the faintest hint of brimstone every time he exhaled.

Then he rose, the weight of him no longer looming over me. Ketch was standing again, hoisted upright far too fast for anything human, like he's used some magic trick that disconnected his bulk from the rules of sinew, gravity, and muscle movement. Sharp talons ripped the tape around my wrist. "Get up," he said. "I've got no further interest in hurting you, right now."

I hesitated, and the order came again, lowered to a feral growl. "Get. Up."

I stood, unsteadily, expecting a trick. Pressed my injured arm close to my chest as the pain settled into a dull throb. I could still see dark shadows at the edge of my vision and my body felt weird, like I'd been made of flesh and helium before getting weight down with bring sparks of agony. Concussion, maybe. In no condition to fight.

It didn't stop me from scanning the floor, searching for the SIG. It was there, half-hidden beneath the coffee table, like we'd kicked the gun there during our scuffle. A temptation. Demons enjoyed doing that. Inviting you to do something stupid and making it seem the sensible, noble option.

Sometimes, a bad option is still the best. I faked a stumble, blocking his view of the gun with my body, slumping into the worn wood of the table. I reached for the SIG left handed, swung it round towards Ketch as I rose.

Ketch shrugged one shoulder, a fire burning in his eyes. The long, muscled frame pulled itself back to full height, and the demon eyed the window, idly scratching at his chest as he sighed. "Shit, seriously?" he said. "You really want to do that, hero? I'm letting you go, you stupid fucker. Free and clear. I'm being generous."

I glanced at the door. Another temptation.

Ketch shook his head. "Get out. I mean it."

My first instinct was to run, flee with all the speed I could manage, but that was the kind of impulse that got you killed. I braced myself, adjusted my grip on the gun.

"Your friend is long gone," Ketch said. "There's no sorcerer worrying at my defenses, nobody tips the scales your way if we pick up the fight. No path to a win here, hero, except trusting me and leaving."

"I tried to kill you."

"And you failed. I'm not holding a grudge."

I didn't believe him. Demons lie, and they hold grudges better than anyone but the fey. Ketch blew an irritated sigh, and I caught the cruel points of his teeth.

"Get out." Ketch said. "Tell Langford she's getting sloppy as hell, and she should play it smarter the next time you try this.

Won't do her any good, but it'll make things amusing. Give me a worthwhile fight, you know?"

I tried to hold the SIG steady and failed. The stupider of the stupid choices almost seemed sensible. I lowered my arm and limped toward the door, waiting for an attack that never came.

SECOND CHANCES

Used to be, when I was a kid, it was easy to find a pay phone. Not so simple anymore, in the age of cheap cells, which hurts like hell when you're limping away from a job gone wrong and your back-ups already absconded with your ride.

These days, when you fuck up, you grit your teeth and lug your aching carcass three kilometres to the nearest Seven-Eleven with a pay phone, then you stand around on the curb until your partner comes to collect you.

Langford didn't say much when she showed up. I stayed quiet the entire way to the Coast, distracting myself from the pain by running through each step of the job, attempting to figure out where it all went wrong. Got as far as the Coomera petrol station before I passed out, didn't come to until we were back on home turf and Langford's skinny arms lugged me into a new safe-house on the twenty-third floor of a holiday resort, down on the beachfront.

Langford made coffee, grabbed a first aid kit from the bathroom. Directed me to the spare bedroom where she started to patch me up. Stitches and antiseptic, to hold my face together. Bandages and a splint, when we got to my arm. I sat there in silence, glaring at her the entire time.

"That was a fucking fiasco," I said.

Langford focused on wrapping my wrist, pulling the bandage tight. "Fucker set up wards we didn't pick up during the surveillance. Didn't help that he was awake to hear us coming."

"Awake I can deal with. Awake is the natural state of most demons, and it's never been a problem. The shit that fucked us was going to work with half the intel missing. That's a recipe for shit going wrong."

"The plan was solid."

"And incomplete."

Lanford caught the accusing tone in my voice, glanced up at me.

"Ketch knew your work," I said. "Claimed you were getting sloppy."

She hit the end of the bandage. Tied it off and stepped back. "That hold?"

I flexed my fingers. The pain was receding with splints and ibuprofen. "It'll do. Sprained?"

Langford nodded, dreadlocks shifting.

"And Ketch?"

She sighed. "You got all kinds of lucky."

"Lucky is escaping. That isn't what happened here. Demons don't offer mercy after a botched hit."

"No," Langford said. "That's true."

I forced my eyes shut and focused on the distant waves, the irregular hiss of them rolling in and thumping against the shore. "Tell me about Cottee."

Harmony snapped the lid of the first aid kit closed. "Gareth's a friend. A good friend."

"And his beef with the demon?"

She sat back against the coffee table and studied her hands. "Ketch is a mistake," she said. "One of mine, and so is Gareth. We groomed him for a time, me and Danny Roark. Gareth was a bright kid who understood the basics of the Gloom, started dabbling with magic. Never going to be a full-fledged sorcerer, but he could pick up enough to do what you do, backed up by someone like Roark. I never wanted to do what you and Danny did together, but Roark convinced me we could do good with Gareth onside."

Harmony cradled the aluminium first aid kit, fingertips rubbing the red cross on the white surface. Moonlight caught the silver stud through her eyebrow as she glanced towards the window. "The shit of it is, I'm not Roark. I taught him a few details, figured he'd keep them to himself, but Cottee experimented. Attempted a few minor rituals. Next thing you know, Gareth's partner is host to a demon…"

Things clicked into place. "Ah. So it's personal."

"Very."

"And you've tried taking care of it before now?"

She nodded. "Me and Gareth, together, and Gareth on his own. We were looking to save him, but as we saw how his power expanded…"

"Yeah, well. Ketch was, what, a friend? A brother?"

"A lover," Langford said. "They were both of them young and stupid, too enamoured of comic books and theories to listen to any warnings I had. Cottee's holding a grudge for what he's lost. Ketch is playing a different game, but make no mistake, if there's anything human left in him…"

"Roark always claimed things go wrong when it gets personal."

Langford's snort ended in a weary choke. "And that asshole never met a job he approached without bias and his own issues stoking his rage."

"Still, he did okay," I said.

"Yeah, I guess he did."

We glared at each other, tired and wary. Waiting for one of us to break.

I huffed and tested my hand. "Could have done this smarter, if you'd told me about the connections."

"We hadn't talked about trying in years. Cottee had gone to ground for a stretch."

"And you figured, what? He'd forget it ever happened?"

"I figured Cottee made peace with it. Turns out, I was wrong," she said. "Ketch wasn't doing much, near as we can tell. He didn't sign-on with any of the local crews, didn't bother trying to recruit other demons. No reason to go after him, beyond Cottee's hard-on. I guessed you'd check things out, see a demon getting by all quiet, was nothing worth fretting about. And then…"

"Then, there was something, and you wanted to try again."

"Ketch is stronger than he was. We needed to move before he became a problem."

"Weeks of surveillance," I said. "Weeks of fucking studying and intel, and this wasn't a detail you bring up?"

"I'm thought I had it handled, no need to talk about it." Langford retreated to the doorway, paused there with one hand resting against the frame. "Listen, we made the attempt. You don't owe me any more than that, and you sure as hell aren't obliged to help Gareth. I'm sorry we didn't warn you of that. Stupid call, but after years of pretending Ketch was harmless… well. Look. Go back to the bar, heal up. I'll figure some other way of taking care of all this."

Tempting. Very fucking tempting.

"Fuck that," I said. "You owe Gareth, I owe you. It's a vicious fucking circle."

I made a tight fist with his right hand, getting used to the pain. "Get Cottee down from Brisbane, tomorrow morning. One thing hasn't changed: we can't let the fucker keep running around."

LOCAL HEROES

We met Cottee in the KFC out on the highway, around the corner from Currumbin Beach. He pulled up in an ancient Honda hatchback, half-rust and half green paint. Climbed and out mopped his forehead, sweaty in the muggy heat. I sat with Langford, watched him shuffle through the car park. The humidity lent him a glossy sheen and half-moons of sweat under his sleeves. I waved him over and he edged closer, hands fluttering as he tried to figure out what to do with them. "Mister Murphy," he said. "It's good to see you."

"Sit." My voice dropped into a growl. Cottee nodded once, eyes on my splint.

"Listen," he said. "I—"

"Ketch is still alive."

His face fell. "Oh."

"Chose not to kill me, and he gave up some interesting hints about his personal history."

"Oh, shit." Cottee wrung his hands together. "I should apologize, I suppose."

"Fuck your apology."

"Please—"

"No." I reached for my paper cup of Pepsi. "What you were hoping for, sending me in there? Tell me what you wanted."

Cottee ground the ball of his thumb into the other hand. "Revenge, maybe. I'm not sure. Holly mentioned what you'd done, prior to ending up here. I figured… perhaps, this time…"

I glared at him, fists bunched, and Cottee's mouth kept working without making noise. Langford touched on my arm, reigned me in. "It's okay," she said. "Just tell him, Gareth."

Cottee looked away. "It wasn't love, if that's what you're wondering. I'll admit we had that once, before I messed around, but I know Ketch isn't the man I fell for. We can't get the human back and the demon is all that remains. Doesn't change the fact I'm the reckless fool who initiated this situation, so call it an obligation, I guess. I owed it to him to fix my mistake. Holly figured—"

"Jesus, you're both idiots." I sipped on my straw and Cottee's eyes flicked from me to Langford, trying to get read.

"I'm sorry," he said. "If you'd like me to leave, I can."

I put my cup down. "Tempting, but we need an expert. You've got an intimate knowledge of the human half, and you know wrestling enough to theorize how to play this to our advantage. I want you to figure something out for me."

Cottee nodded.

"Why did Ketch let me go?"

"I don't—"

"We botched it," I said. "Three rounds hurt him, but he didn't stay down. Nor did he rip me apart like most demons would in that situation. Instead, he asked me to leave with my gun. Ketch practically dared me and Langford to attempt another hit. That isn't normal."

Cottee frowned. Nodded. "For demons, no."

"For wrestling?"

He shrugged. "It's what bad guys do," he said. "There's a tradition in wrestling, when you're trying to get a heel over. You send a guy out there, every show, to make an open challenge. Let him bring in unknown, hometown guys for a last-five-minutes-and-you'll-win-a-prize kind of thing. Except no-one really lasts the time limit. Your heel goes out there and murder opponents every show."

He raised a hand, forestalling questions. "Metaphorically killed, I mean. Submission holds and pain and…"

He trailed off, frowning. "Beating on the local boy makes the crowd hate 'em, and heels loathed by the fans are the lifeblood of the industry. The potential of seeing them get their comeuppance lures people in every week. Except they don't. Weeks go by. Months, sometimes. Or years. You stoke the fire until you're ready to make a new golden boy and push him up the card. He answers the challenge, but he doesn't get to win. Just lasts the five minutes, first guy to do so, and even then he's beaten-up after the bell rings."

"I certainly feel beat-up," I said.

Cottee met the joke with a wan smile. "The golden boy's the guy who feuds with the heel, gets a series of matches where the heel wins dirty to fan the flames a little more. Promoter waits until biggest show they've got is coming, and that's when the hero tips the odds in his favor. No holds barred, no time limit, the whole match inside a cage. Doesn't matter how, so long as you signal this is the moment the audience is waiting for. Your new golden boy pins the unbeatable arsehole and become a big damn hero."

I understood about half of Cottee's explanation, but the repeated phrases stood out. "Ketch started calling me Hero when he ranted at me."

"Okay. That makes sense." Cottee paused and sucked in a steady breath. "You've been beat," he said, "and you're still kicking. Ketch is drawing strength from that, like he does inside the ring. Transposing structures from the ritual of combat into a real fight. Might be he's saving you up. Build up a rematch, so it means more when he kills you."

"Except the bad guys get beat in wrestling, in the end, and I didn't last five minutes."

Cottee's fingers drummed the table. "This is all just a theory."

"It's a starting point to work with." Langford grinned. "And I've got an idea."

"I don't owe you enough to die," I said.

"Sure you do." Her grin widened a little. "Shouldn't come to that, though. We go back to first principles: locations matter. Symbols matter. If he's drawing power from the rituals of wrestling, we can do something with that. Get you an audience and a ring…"

I looked to Cottee. "Location matters, in this thing?"

"It does. Whole things about local heroes breaking out."

"Could we use it to our advantage?"

Cottee's nervous hands grew still. "We could, but I don't rate your chances. You can't wade in there with guns to fight him, not if we're playing it by wrestling rules. You'll have to engage on the same terms as the ritual, and that means… well, you know, fisticuffs."

Cottee threw a couple of punches at the air. They looked like crap.

"New plan, then," I said. "No way I'm taking on a demon bare-handed." I held up my splint. "Especially not with this."

"Then we'll arm you." Langford grinned as she pieced a concept together. "Take the sword and use it."

"Any weapon would be an illegal," Cottee said. "And good guys fight clean. Wrestling logic 101. The only time they cheat is when the heel cheats first, pushing the face to a point of frustration. Even then, giving into the temptation and stooping to their level—"

"So you're saying I'm allowed to cross the line, so long as Ketch crosses it before me?"

Cottee scrunched his forehead, mulling it over. "More or less."

"We can work with that."

REMATCH

The sword was three feet of dull, serviceable metal we'd stolen from the deepest parts of the Gloom. The kind of weapon with a dozen mythological names, if you traced its history of making appearances in our world. Cottee would have a term for it, rave about its metaphoric resonance with every magic blade ever swung in the name of doing good. Me, I used it to stab people, and even then I hated the damn thing. Swords were a bad idea, no matter which way you sliced it. Any weapon that needed you up-close and personal with your enemy gave the other guy far too many opportunities to kill you first.

I preferred to shoot things. It played to my strengths. But you repay debts in this line of work, and that meant digging the sword out of the lock-box hidden beneath my office desk.

I sat in the driver's seat of Gareth Cottee's hatchback, studying the gym where Ketch and his fellow wrestlers assembled to train each Thursday. It didn't look like much, just a stainless-steel shed in the middle of an industrial estate, a small lot out the front for regulars. We'd been staking the place out for a few hours, waiting for the trainees to leave. Cottee checked his watch, nodded to himself. "It's time."

He was pale beneath the perspiration. I couldn't blame him. Sweat prickled my neck as I exited the car, hauled the sheathed sword out of the back seat and slung it over my shoulder. It was getting dark, shadows growing longer as the sun set. A poster by the shed door advertised their next show, three days away. I glanced over at Cottee. "Ready?"

He didn't really nod, just inclined his head a little. He led the way, not bothering with anything like stealth as we barged into the wrestling gym. The faint sourness of too much sweat clung to the walls and canvas. Ketch worked out up the back, lifting weights. He looked up as we entered, his arms still moving in a smooth rhythm, muscles bunching beneath his grubby singlet. "Gareth and the hero. Two people who should have known better."

"Some of us learn slow." I gestured to the ring. "You interested in a rematch?"

Ketch's lip curled. "Gareth's been talking, I see."

"That's not a yes."

Ketch smirked and loped over, smooth and graceful as a jungle cat. I climbed up the apron and clambered through the ropes. Handed the sword to Cottee and turned towards the demon on the floor. "No guns, this time," I said. "We do it by the rules."

Ketch stepped to the centre of the ring and offered a mocking handshake.

"Wait!" Gareth's voice squeaked, pitch rising higher than any man his size should achieve.

Ketch's laughed rolled across the ring. "Gareth, love, did you just attempt an order?"

"Light it up." Gareth's speech grew steady, and he locked eyes with Ketch. "You want an opponent, you want an audience, I'm giving you both. Do it right and light up the ring."

A bare bulb flared to life, illuminating the red and blue cables running from the ring posts. Ketch dropped his barbell and loped up to the apron, sneer growing deeper with each step. "Is that true, hero? You demand a rematch?"

"You saying no?"

"Stupid," Ketch said. "Your injured. You left your sorceress at home. You left your guns behind. This is my house, my ring."

"I'll risk it.".

"Then I accept."

I didn't see Ketch move, not really. Just a flicker of movement in the corner of my eye, a blur as he charged. Then something hard and unyielding smashed against my jaw, sent me reeling back into the ropes. The impact rolled through my life the flash-wave of a bomb, a precursor to the pain that followed in its wake. I groped for turnbuckles, used them to stay upright. Another fist hooked into my stomach, doubling me over. Strong hands hoisted me, twisted and slammed me into the mat. Ketch grated my cheek against the canvas, opening up my stitches.

I swung a wild elbow, caught him in the face. Ketch backed off, just a little, gave me space to clamber to my feet. There wasn't anything slick about my approach, nothing stylized or graceful. I threw desperate fists, hammered Ketch hard as I could. He retreated, circling left, grinning the entire way. I followed, half-stumbling, struggling to put power behind a blow. Tagged him below the right eye and his skin broke, blood seeping free.

Ketch grabbed my injured arm and twisted it against my back, the pain leveraging me to my knees. He dragged my dead weight to ringside and jammed me against the apron. "You're lazy, hero, and you're not built for this."

Splinters from the wooden splint dug into my wrist. I cried out, grabbing the ropes with my other hand. Tried to kick my way free with both legs.

Ketch slapped me across the face. "Get up," he said.

I got up on the balls of my feet, just like Danny Roark taught me. Swung a few times without connection before Ketch put a boot into my stomach. I went down hard and his bulk crashed into me, both hands locking around my throat. Hot breath pressed against my ear. "I applaud your persistence, hero. It's worth more, killing you here. Far better than snapping your neck in my kitchen."

I gasped, my face burning. Desperate to break free. Ketch cinched his choke a little tighter, squeezing the life out of me.

"Toby."

Ketch faltered, gave me a moment to catch my breath.

"Toby, stop," Cottee said. He was up on the apron, pleading with the demon. "This isn't you, man. This isn't—"

Ketch planted a right against Cottee's jaw and knocked him to the floor. The big academic's weight slapped concrete hard. No doubt it would hurt like hell in the morning, maybe even do permanent damage.

I crawled to the corner, collected the sword. Pulled it from the sheath.

Ketch laughed, spreading his arms wide. "Breaking the rules, hero-boy."

"Chokes illegal. You broke 'em first."

Ketch's laughter picked up volume. I didn't bother talking anymore, charged in and buried the point of the sword deep into his chest. Ketch snarled, stumbling backwards. Sagged against the ropes. Wet blood stained the canvas, joining my own. Ketch swung at me, a wild haymaker that knocked me to the floor. I landed on my right shoulder, felt something pop that shouldn't.

I forced myself upright, stabbed again. The fire in Ketch's eyes snuffed out, and he sank to his knees, trying to hold his guts in.

Gareth Cottee's rapid breathing echoed in the darkness, the

big man scrambling through the bottom rope. "Toby," he whimpered. "Shit, Toby."

Ketch sucked desperate breaths, attempting to staunch the blood flow. I tried to pull the sword free, stab him again, but Ketch's blood-slick hand grabbed at my wrist. The demon reached for Cottee, fixing the big man with an angry stare. "Not Toby. Not anymore," it hissed.

Cottee closed his eyes, tears spilling down his cheeks.

"Watch," Ketch said. "This needs an audience."

Rules. Always rules with demons and magic.

I jerked out of Ketch's grip and his fingers left bloody smears against my forearm. The demon reared back, hoping to bludgeon me across the head with both fists. I took the opening and stabbed, the sword digging in blow his ribcage and sliding through the chest. I twisted the blade for good measure, and blood slicked over my arm. Ketch screamed, and Cottee winced at the noise, but the academic held steady. His puffy eyes stayed open and focused.

Ketch dropped to both knees and coughed twice. I hauled the sword free and stabbed him again.

"Enough." Cottee's muted voice barely registered on me. I drew the sword back and stabbed a third time.

"Enough," Cottee repeated, louder this time. There were tears dribbling into his beard. "It's done, Mister Murphy. He's gone."

WINNER, AND NEW CHAMPION

I put through a call to Langford. "Jobs done."

"Good. One less you owe me," she said, and I agreed, that was true. She tried another apology for fucking me around and I hung up the phone.

Gareth Cottee waited out front, slumped up against his SUV. Nobody around to notice his red eyes and panicked sniffle, nor the gore slicked down my arm. That's the nice thing about industrial estates: only folks who come out there at night were occasional security patrols, and their appearance meant you'd tripped an alarm.

I limped over, wrist pressed close to my chest, and sagged against the car beside Cottee. "You okay?"

Cottee blinked at me. "Yeah," he said. "No. It's possible I'm not sure."

"I get that." It hurt to hobble my way to the passenger side and force aching fingers to open the door. "You think you're right to drive?"

He nodded, but Cottee fumbled his keys when he pulled them from his pocket. They clattered against the concrete, and he jumped at the noise. Part of me wished I could take over for the poor bastard, give him time to process everything he'd seen. Instead, I needed to re-splint my arm, swallow a metric ton of painkillers, and sleep for half a week.

"Well then," I said. "Before anyone arrives."

Cottee gathered his keyring and huddled in the driver's set. Struggled with the gearstick as he tried to move into third, although he got it there eventually and started winding his way out towards the highway. My right arm burned the entire trip, fresh pain blooming any time I shifted in my seat. My shoulder protested as loud as the wrist, now. That wasn't a good sign. "Every instinct I have tells me to bug out of town," I said. "First rule of hitting things from the Gloom, get clear before the death curses start."

Cottee answered in a low, hollow voice. "Demons don't have death curses."

"No, but they leave corpses. They attract cops."

"Oh," Cottee said. "Yeah, I guess they do."

We drove four blocks without saying a thing. Cottee searched the radio band, kept skipping past the stations and listening to the empty static. He sniffled and wiped his nose with a sleeve.

"First time I ever ran," I said, "I left a girl behind. Figured it was necessary. No real choice. Took comfort in that for years, until circumstances sent me home again." I shifted. Winced. Transferred my attention to the window and the streets of Brisbane rolling past. "Didn't end all that well, after we reconnected. Leaving might not have been the best thing for her."

"I heard she attempted to kill you."

"Lot of old friends tried that when I came back. Wasn't unique to her."

That earned me a weak smile amid that heavy beard. "Not the same as killing her, though."

"No, I guess it ain't."

Cottee followed the road out onto the highway. Followed the highway south, to the Gold Coast. Neither of us said another thing the entire way home.

STORY NOTES

LOVE IS THE ROAR OF A CHAINSAW, CUTTING FLESH IN THE NIGHT

If I were a musician who released albums, rather than a writer, this collection would likely come with the subtitle *B-Sides and Rarities*. The stories published here are a motley assemblage compared to my first two collections, and draws upon publications in some hard-to-find anthologies, out-of-print omnibus editions, or magazines that have closed their doors.

This story may be one of the rarest of rarities. In 2014 the creators of a mobile game, Dead End Alley, commissioned four Australian horror authors to write a piece from the same prompt: *A blind alley, a swarm of hungry zombies, a chainsaw, and you.*

This was my contribution, published on Facebook and the Dead End Alley webpage alongside stories from Alan Baxter, Kaaron Warren, and Deborah Biancotti.

Around the time I wrote this two of my closest friends were in the process of assembling their own survival kit, and they'd just informed me the American Center for Disease Control and Preventions hosted zombie preparedness guidelines on its website. They're definitely worth a Google if you haven't read them—it never hurts to prepare.

ONE LAST FIRST DATE BEFORE THE END OF THE WORLD

This story began with a challenge challenged to write a story based on a random word, and mine was limerence—the state of mind that results from romantic attraction and the desire to form a relationship and have one's feelings reciprocated. It's also known as the first three months of dating, when you're figuring things out and drunk on the dopamine hit, eager to spend all your time together. The period where certain traits get overlooked in the rush, even if they might serve as warning signs a few months down the track.

It might seem like the end of the world seemed is a pretty big thing to overlook while in the limerence state, but I would argue that humanity is fantastic at ignoring looming threats of extinction in general.

COUNTING DOWN

Some short stories have interesting origins, worthy of becoming tales unto themselves. I've written stories based on a dare, or because I wanted to prove someone wrong, or because *friends have told me a certain story needed to exist* but wasn't out there yet.

This isn't one of those—it's the result of listening to The Birthday Party's Release the Bats on repeat and not getting a lot of sleep. There is only so long that combination can continue before you start wondering where the bats are being released from...

THE PLACE BEYOND THE BRAMBLES

Originally inspired by a piece from the Australian artist Terry Whidborne, produced for a short story project from the Brisbane-based Tiny Owl Workshop. Through various trials and tribulations, it ended up being published at Daily Science Fiction instead.

While Tiny Owl didn't publish this story, they're responsible for producing the most unique publication in my publishing history. In 2013 they commissioned work for their Pillow Fight! project, seeking out flash fictions they'd print onto the cushions used at the Brisbane Writers Festival lounge later that year. This is my story, originally printed on a large pillow, now presented here as a little bonus for people who enjoy reading Story Notes.

JUST ANOTHER NIGHT OF BAD DECISIONS

Hal Tucker was one of those guys, you know? Ugly and unpleasant, but he had a magnetic presence. I figured him for an all-right bloke.

I was out back, on smoko, when I heard the news.

"You hear old Tucker got himself gutted?" Mitch sat on the steps and tapped free a cigarette, lighting it with a flourish. "They found him down in the park this morning. Someone tore his guts open and played cats-cradle with his intestines."

I stopped eating and pushed the plate away. Mitch Roy was a prick in every way that mattered. He considered himself *The Man* 'cause he managed a joint on the Gold Coast strip. I work part time at his restaurant as a short-order cook, 'cause there isn't exactly a steady career in freelance occultism. Mitch took up my discarded plate and started picking at the leftover chunks of beef in the madras.

I don't remember what I said in return—I was too busy thinking. I'd seen Tucker down by the underpass two days ago, another crazy burn-out. He'd offered me a sword and the chance to stand vigil with him, face down whatever evils passed into this world. I told him maybe some other time, when I wasn't so shagged from working. Now, it was too late. Something bad got him, and I'd shirked my duty.

I stood, wiped my hands on my apron. "Listen, Mitch, I gotta go."

"Like hell," Mitch said. "You're halfway through your shift."

"It's important," I said.

Mitch shrugged. He didn't believe in magic, didn't believe in much beyond women and smokes, really. "Go," he said, "and you're gone for good."

I stayed. I needed the job.

They found Mitch floating in the canals later that night.

He should have let me go hunting the werewolves, I guess.

THE THINGS YOU DO WHEN THE WAR BREAKS OUT

My friend, Kathleen Jennings, will occasionally take the weird diversions that twitter conversations amble down and transform them into small, post-it note illustrations. One week, after a discussion about the history of flight, dinosaurs, and Terrance Haile's *Space Train*, she came up with a quick sketch that fused the three.

I started wondering about the people on the train, and why the pterodactyls were there, and somewhere along the line the story took a far darker turn than expected.

WINGED, WITH SHARP TEETH

Another story inspired by a Kathleen Jennings twitter sketch, this time a winged crocodile with a particularly smug grin. You can still see it online, if Twitter hasn't yet self-destructed in whatever timeline you read this.

I started this story years ago, writing paragraphs on my lunch break at work. I finished in 2019 while my father was in the hospital—the first of several trips. At the time, I wasn't truly conscious of how much his Parkinson's and growing dementia had become part of the background noise of our family life. Looking back on the early drafts, after his death, it seems incredibly obvious.

UPON DISCOVERING A GHOST IN THE FIVE STAR

I was in a slump where nothing I wrote worked properly and needed a quick break. I spun up some online writing prompts and amused myself by writing quick, goofy flash pieces based on whatever I found.

One prompt was visual: a photograph of a young, pale girl

with a balloon in her hands. It wasn't a big jump to transform her into a ghost, and I'd been making notes about a series of laundromat stories for years. What started as fun writing exercise quickly expanded into a full story.

One day, I'll finish the next three entries in the Laundromat series.

TITHES

Jennifer Brozek was putting together an anthology about magic Hobo Nickels and needed a pinch hitter to fill a gap. She asked if I could put together a 5,000 word story about a coin bringing misery to the protagonist in the next five days.

It's rare that I can finish anything that fast from a standing start, but I wanted to give it a shot. Unfortunately, it was the week I started my only full-time office job, which meant running on very little sleep in order to get the story done.

Tithes shares the universe of my Keith Murphy stories, themselves published in two separate projects helmed by Brozek. While Nate, Byron, and Angela are dealing with their own problems, the real joy was bringing in one of my favourite Keith Murphy supporting characters—the demon Randall—and letting him play saviour rather than the villain.

THE MINOTAURS & THE SIGNAL GHOSTS

Written for Robin Laws *The Lion and the Aardvark*, an anthology of contemporary fables building on the traditions of Aesop. I skipped ahead to write a fable from a cyberpunk future instead.

HORNETS ATTACK YOUR BEST FRIEND VICTOR AND OTHER THINGS WE CALLED THE BAND

My partner's favourite superhero is Dazzler, and I like writing horror stories about the Gold Coast. We weren't dating yet, but I wanted to write something she might enjoy.

It's also an attempt to capture the experience of seeing art-focused bands such as The Dirty Three or The Paradise Motel play venues in the heart of the Gold Coast's tourist districts, and a lament for the various live music clubs that have disappeared over the years.

EIGHT MINUTES OF USABLE DAYLIGHT

A story with its beginnings in tabletop roleplaying games, such as Dungeons and Dragons, where the idea of liquid sunlight is just another day at the office for vampire-hunting adventurers and cities cloaked in eternal darkness are a staple backdrop.

Like most D&D things, the real fun comes when you remove them from their original context and start asking questions.

THE MIKE & CARLY STORY, WITHOUT THE GOSSIP

This is an enormously fun story to read aloud, and it's been my go-to for public events ever since it was first published in the late, lamented *Shimmer* magazine.

I wrote it to experiment with the narrative voice and the power of a narrator who both speaks directly to the reader and engages in editorialising as the story progresses. It's a friendly kind of story, and it makes me happy every time I come across it.

A WHITE CROSS BESIDE A LONELY ROAD

I wrote the first draft while attending Clarion South back in 2007, trying my hand a ghost story. It was a step outside my comfort zone, and the feedback was generally positive, but suggested it needed something more—an edge that made it stand out, or a bit more depth to the story. It didn't feel like anything else I'd written across the six week's we spent together and didn't fit with a lot of the other stuff I'd written around that time.

I wrote the final draft nearly a decade later, while taking Neil Gaiman's online Masterclass and experimenting with the exercises he used to refine an idea and develop it. I'm not sure why I chose to revisit A White Cross Beside A Lonely Road, but I expect it's because it's a story that had given me trouble for so long.

It caught me by surprise when I opened a fresh page of my notebook and started working on it again, because the process unearthed a bunch of things about Alex and Brendan that had never quite appeared on the page before and showed me who they really were.

This may be a ghost story, but it's not really about the ghost—what interested me is the way people get haunted by the expectations of others and judge their life by those standards.

RULE 34

Written for Heather Wood's *Gods, Memes, & Monsters: a 21st Century Bestiary* about magical and mythological creatures in the present day.

At the time I was teaching workshops about using the internet as a writer, talking aspiring writers through the things they could be learning from things like fanfic and online publishing, and I'd frequently get reminders of just how accurate Rule 34 of the internet truly is: if you can imagine it, there is porn based on it.

And mythology already had a race of creatures known for wish fulfilment…

LOCAL HEROES

A story that exists because of my deep, affirming love of professional wrestling, which truly is more absurd and wonderful than most folks give it credit for. Every time folks try to explain that wrestling is fake, I point out the number of shows I've enjoyed featuring wrestling demons, wrestling vampires, wrestling bees, wrestling wizards, wrestling wombats, and imaginary hand grenades.

If you assume people watch pro-wrestling like it's real, you're obviously not paying attention.

I wrote a short, truncated version of this story as part of the first, serialised incarnation of Keith Murphy's adventures. This expanded version emerged as a bonus story for Apocalypse Ink's hardcover omnibus of the Keith Murphy novellas, *Flotsam*, representing a first glimpse at what Keith would be up to after the fight to prevent Ragnarök.

PUBLICATION HISTORY

Several of these stories have appeared elsewhere, in some cases in a different form:

- "Love is the Roar of a Chainsaw, Cutting Flesh in the Night" © 2014 Peter M. Ball. First published on the Dead End Alley Facebook page
- "Hornets Attack Your Best Friend Victor & Other Things We Called The Band" © 2017 Peter M. Ball. First published in *Speculate*, February 2017
- "The Place Beyond The Brambles" © 2015 Peter M. Ball. First published in *Daily Science Fiction*, November 2015
- "One Last First Date Before The End Of the World" © 2019 Peter M. Ball. First published in *Short Fiction Lab #4*, 2019
- "The Things You Do When The War Breaks Out" © 2016 Peter M. Ball. First published in *Daily Science Fiction*, December 2016
- "Winged, With Sharp Teeth" © 2019 Peter M. Ball. First published in *Short Fiction Lab #1*, 2019.
- "Upon Discovering A Ghost In The Five Star" © 2016 Peter M. Ball. First published in *Daily Science Fiction*, June 2016

ACKNOWLEDGEMENTS

First, my heartfelt thanks to my family: my mother, Margaret Ball; my sister, Sally Ball; my father, Terry Ball; and my partner, Sarah Hobday. Your support makes so much of this possible.

Thanks also to my parents in crime at Write Club, Angela Slatter and Kathleen Jennings, where so many of these stories were drafted.

Thanks to the editors who commissioned my stories for anthologies: Jennifer Brozek, Robin Laws, and Heather Woods.

The staff and student body of the Griffith University Creative Writing program, who gave me the opportunity to both learn about the short story and teach others about them as well (and really, teaching is just another kind of learning).

The team of Queensland Writers Centre., where I worked as so many of these stories were being written, and whose influence still guides my career today.

ABOUT THE AUTHOR

PETER M. BALL is an author, publisher, and RPG gamer whose love of speculative fiction emerged after exposure to *The Hobbit*, *Star Wars*, David Lynch's *Dune*, and far too many games of *Dungeons and Dragons* before the age of 7. He's spent the bulk of his life working as a creative writing tutor, with brief stints as a performance poet, gaming convention organiser, online content developer, non-profit arts manager, GenreCon convenor, and d20 RPG publisher.

He's the author of the Miriam Aster series and the Keith Murphy Urban Fantasy Thrillers, three short story collections, and more stories, articles, poems, and RPG material than he'd care to count.

He's the brain-in-charge at Brain Jar Press, an aspiring made scientist running publishing experiments through Eclectic Projects, and resides in Brisbane, Australia, with his partner and a very affectionate cat.

Find Peter Online at PeterMBall.com *or reach out to Peter on your favourite Social Media platforms:*

patreon.com/PeterMBall

facebook.com/PeterMBall

instagram.com/PeterMBall

twitter.com/PeterMBall

tiktok.com/@petermball

goodreads.com/PeterMBall

bookbub.com/authors/peter-m-ball

ALSO BY PETER M. BALL

SHORT STORY COLLECTIONS

The Birdcage Heart & Other Strange Tales

Not Quite The End Of the World Just Yet: Short Stories & Strange Futures

These Strange & Magic Things: Short Stories

KEITH MURPHY URBAN FANTASY THRILLERS

Exile

Frost

Crusade

Local Heroes

Gold Coast Ragnarok (Omnibus)

MIRIAM ASTER NOVELLAS

Horn

Bleed

BRAIN JAR PRESS SHORT FICTION LAB

The Early Experiments

Winged, With Sharp Teeth

8 Minutes Of Usable Daylight

A White Cross Beside A Lonely Road

One Last First Date Before The End Of The World

Shedding Skins

ESSAYS

You Don't Want To Be Published & Other Things Nobody Tells You When You First Start Writing

CHAPBOOKS

Deeper Cuts: Night, Morning, Story & Impact

Gold Coast, 2002: Poems

THANK YOU!

I'd like to extend my thanks to the following incredible people who supported Eclectic Projects via Patreon. Their support is a big reason this book — and these stories — exists.

Margaret Ball
Kate Eltham
Jodi
Nicole Strickland
Meg Vann
Sally
Jennifer White
Maggie Slater
Tansy Rayner Roberts
Dave Versace
Mark Webb
Catherine Caine
Kathleen Jennings
Stephanie Gunn
Lois Spangler

Thank you all!

NEWSLETTER SIGN-UP

Be the first to know!

Sign up for the Peter M. Ball newsletter to and you'll get the latest news on releases and deals, plus an ebook starter library and the occasional give away.

What are you waiting for? Sign up at
petermball.com/newsletter